Caroline gazed into the hearth and imagined the firelight shimmering on his dark hair and the reddish glow from the flames dancing on his face. She could picture his intent blue eyes beckoning to her. In seconds, she would find herself enveloped in his strong arms. Just before the fiery embers flickered out, he would tenderly cradle her face and kiss her, murmuring the words she so longed to hear.

Oh, Matt . . . how I wish you were here tonight. . . .

Dear Readers,

We at Silhouette would like to thank all our readers for your many enthusiastic letters. In direct response to your encouragement, we are now publishing *three* FIRST LOVEs every month.

As always FIRST LOVEs are written especially for and about you—your hopes, your dreams, your ambitions.

Please continue to share your suggestions and comments with us; they play an important part in our pleasing you.

I invite you to write to us at the address below:

Nancy Jackson
Senior Editor
Silhouette Books
P.O. Box 769
New York, N.Y. 10019

ALL-AMERICAN GIRL
Vanessa Payton

First Love from Silhouette

Published by Silhouette Books New York

America's Publisher of Contemporary Romance

SILHOUETTE BOOKS, a Simon & Schuster Division of
GULF & WESTERN CORPORATION
1230 Avenue of the Americas, New York, N.Y. 10020

ISBN: 0-671-53338-X

First Silhouette Books printing February, 1983

10 9 8 7 6 5 4 3 2 1

America's Publisher of Contemporary Romance

Printed in the U.S.A.

For my Val—
For all her support
And for unselfishly sharing
her world with me,
Much Love

ALL-AMERICAN GIRL

1

Caroline Vickers was always nervous before a game. It didn't matter what sport it was—basketball, tennis, or like now, field hockey. It was always the same. Before every game she felt like a zillion butterflies were playing follow the leader around her stomach and up her throat. But she had every right to be nervous. This was the state championships and the Glendale Chargers were here! She still couldn't believe it. For years, Glendale's hockey team stayed in the league's basement. If you couldn't beat the Chargers "you were hurtin' for certain," the saying went. It was only in the last two years that the team had improved. Improved? What a laugh. Tying for fifth place in a league of seven teams wasn't much of an improvment and last year they had come in fourth. But this year was different. Something had happened. The Chargers weren't laughed at anymore. They won and won until they climbed to second place in their league. What a party they had the night of their victory! Caroline drank so much punch she thought she would float home but the celebration hadn't ended then. The next day banners and signs greeted the team at the school—courtesy of the other female athletes and gym instructors, Caroline was sure. The student body went wild. Even the school paper did a special issue on the team and her in particular. As high scorer for the game with three goals, Caroline was a celebrity. She also held the honor of being high scorer for the season. She scored fourteen goals of her own that year and had four assists to her credit because her passing set up four more goals by her teammates. Now the Chargers were at the state championship. And she was sick as a dog.

"Caroline, are you all right?"

Taking a breather from her stretching exercises, Caroline looked directly in the eyes of her coach.

"I feel rotten. I think I'm going to die!"

With a quick laugh and knowing smile Barbara Peters put an arm around her star athlete. She had coached Caroline for the first time that season, but how many times had she heard this from her before a game? She couldn't remember. All she knew was it didn't matter. Caroline was as green as a frog before each; once the action started she was all business.

"You'll be fine, Caroline. Just relax and take a couple of deep breaths."

Nodding to her coach, Caroline did as instructed.

While watching her young charge, Coach Peters knew she was looking at a winner. Ability, endurance, and dedication. The signs were all there. Yes, she's one of the chosen few, Coach Peters thought. She could be great. She's only a sophomore now but with a little more work she could have her choice of athletic scholarships. But she's got to settle down.

"How're the jitters now, Caroline?" Coach Peters asked.

"Under control, coach."

"Great! Okay, kids," the coach shouted to her team. "Let's do some windsprints, please."

*   *   *

The "rust bucket" was in rare form. Coach Peters' '75 Ford wagon had definitely seen better days and better shock absorbers too.

Jostled, tossed, and generally battered with each turn and dip in the road, Caroline could barely sit upright. Of course the poking and prodding Beth and Sheila were giving her wasn't helping matters. But sandwiched between her two friends in the middle seat with the rest of her teammates around and behind her, Caroline felt even a ride in a sleek Lincoln Continental couldn't be any better, for they were winners! The Glendale Chargers were now the number one team in the state.

The sound of the final whistle had caused pandemonium to break out as Caroline and her teammates hugged and cried with happiness over their victory. Even Coach Peters couldn't contain her happiness as the tears rolled freely down her cheeks. It was a grand occasion. There were many who would say it was a miracle. But those who followed the game gave much of the credit to the slim, laughing figure in the middle enjoying the easy camaraderie of friends and teammates.

"Hey, Slim. *What happened to you* at the end of the game?" a voice from the rear yelled with staccato emphasis.

Almost five feet eight and slender, "Slim" had been Caroline's nickname for as long as she could remember. She just seemed to hit her growth spurt before her fellow classmates had. Even if it hadn't been her height, Caroline's wavy, abundant, ash brown hair and grey-green eyes would have garnered her more than her share of attention in a crowd.

"Well, what happened? Where'd you get that 'get up and go'?"

Hoots and whistles greeted that question, for everyone jammed into the old station wagon knew what was meant. Despite quick passing and good play throughout the game, the score remained a one-all tie for most of the contest. Then in the closing five minutes of play, Caroline scored two quick goals, stunning the opposition and the Charger fans as well.

"Well, what happened?"

Caroline recognized the persistent voice as belonging to Katie Hollis. "Loud and wild—but really a nice girl," Caroline's mother always said of Katie. Katie was nonetheless a natural leader and one of the best liked girls on the team. Besides she was team captain, which didn't hurt her popularity any.

"I don't know," Caroline innocently replied while rolling her eyes heavenward. "I was just so mad when that girl playing halfback *accidentally* tripped me—*twice*," she said sarcastically and with little laughter, "that all I could think of was getting even."

"Well, two quick goals in five minutes is the best way to get even I ever heard of."

Cheers and applause followed Katie's comments, and Caroline could do nothing but blush, which only intensified the razzing her friends gave her.

Embarrassed and practically on the floor from the pounding she was receiving, a quick stop to let out some of the passengers bounced her into the air briefly and against the front seat. Between the ecstatic pounding of her comrades, the exertion of the game itself, and the bumpy ride home, Caroline knew she would be as stiff as a board and bruised beyond description; but she didn't care. The Glendale Chargers were truly winners at last! And she was the star of the game.

As the wagon made the right-hand turn unto Meetinghouse Lane, Caroline gathered her hockey equipment. Maple and white birch trees lined the avenue, practically arcing over the street itself. The Vickers homestead was like many of its neighbors—pre–World War II, large, a monster to heat, but they loved it too much to sell. Recently they had glass-enclosed the back porch and installed there a wood burning stove for extra heat so that they could use the porch during the colder months of the year. Caroline had always thought of her house as being very friendly. Neatly trimmed evergreen bushes lined the flagstone walk leading to the front door. The green shutters opening on the white facade gave the house a warm welcoming appearance, she thought. She couldn't imagine living anywhere else. Going away to college would not be easy for her, she knew, but there was time enough before that happened.

As the Ford came to a lumbering halt in front of her home, Caroline unsteadily stepped out and said goodbye to her friends. This was the last hockey season for the seniors unless they continued in college. But the friendships Caroline had found on the team wouldn't end with the field hockey season. There were classes and numerous social events such as the Sadie Hawkins Dance just a month away. There was still lots of fun and good times in store for all of them.

Swinging her gym bag over her shoulders, Caroline began to run up the walk.

"Caroline!"

Amidst the din of the raucous celebration taking place in the wagon behind her, she had barely heard her name called. Turning around in midstride, she saw Coach Peters leaning out the front passenger window with her hand extended.

Taller than Caroline by inches, Barbara Peters' curly blond hair blew gently in the evening's breeze. It was still hard for Caroline to believe she was twenty-eight years old and married, for the coach had the face and trim physique to rival any of her students.

"I'm really proud of you," Coach Peters said as she clasped Caroline's hand. "It took determination and drive to do what you did." Her voice turned serious. "I'm glad you went out for the team this year. You'll go far in athletics if you keep up that attitude."

Caroline felt her eyes misting as she listened to her coach's kind words. This was high praise from someone she respected and admired. "Thanks, coach," she said shakily. Then with a jaunty last wave to her friends she turned once more toward her home.

Striding into the front foyer, Caroline wasn't in the house for more than three seconds before she heard the tapping of little paws in the upstairs hallway. Quickly she tossed her belongings in the foyer closet but before she could hide, her pet cocker spaniel ran down the stairs and began to bark the house down.

"Sleeping on my bed again?" Caroline said in mock anger. Responding to her mistress's tone of voice, the small, tawny gold ball of energy fell silent and tilted her head questioningly. Amber had been Caroline's birthday gift two years ago and since then, she wondered more than once how she ever lived without her before. As Caroline clapped her hands and whistled, the spaniel leapt into her arms and began licking her face with relish.

"Oh, Amber," she crooned into the dog's ear. "We won! We won! Isn't that wonderful?"

"Carrie! . . . Caroline! Is that you?" It was her mother's voice.

"Yesssss, it's me," She carried Amber with her into the dining room where Mrs. Vickers was folding peach cotton napkins and placing them under the silverware already arranged at four place settings.

"Where have you been? It's almost eight o'clock. I expected you home a long time ago to help with the dinner." Then spying Caroline's furry passenger she said in exasperation, "Do you mind getting her *away* from the table, please. She's the only dog I know who still sheds in the fall and personally I can do without her hair on *my* plate. Thank you."

Stroking Amber's fur once more Caroline deposited her in the doorway leading to the living room. Then wrapping her arms around herself in a gesture she often used when hurt or caught in the wrong, she followed her mother into the kitchen. Invisible lint seemed to occupy her as she picked at the hem of her green plaid kilt.

"I'm sorry, mom. The team had a big celebration after the game tonight. It was the last game of the season and everybody was having such a good time nobody wanted to leave."

"Oh, Caroline," Mrs. Vickers began apologetically. "I should have known that's where you were."

"That's okay, mom. I should have reminded you before I left this morning. I was just in such a hurry, I forgot."

Smiling, Mrs. Vickers stroked her daughter's hair and gave her a quick hug. They were a very demonstrative family. Caroline's older brother Kurt always said they were the "touchiest, feeliest bunch" he had ever come across.

"Welll—aren't you going to give me a blow-by-blow account of the game? How did you do?" her mother asked.

"We won, mom! I scored two goals! We're number one in the state! Do you believe it?"

Mrs. Vickers knew better than to attempt to answer her daughter. Besides, once Caroline started talking she rattled louder than a tambourine. Mrs. Vickers' eyes glowed with pride as she listened to her daughter recount the game and her role in it.

"I'm very happy for you, honey. Wait till your father hears. He'll be thrilled," she continued, as she removed the roast duck from the oven. "And I know you're glad it's all over. I mean I'm sure you've had fun but now you'll have more time for your studies and other friends."

Oh no, Caroline thought, a frown creasing her smooth clear brow. Here we go again. I know what "other friends" means. It means guys and girls who don't participate in sports.

Caroline couldn't understand her mother. She was practically a "women's libber," yet when it came to Caroline's playing sports her mother was always against it. Caroline could never understand why. Her older sister, Bobbie, had been a cheerleader which had pleased her mother to no end. True, cheerleading wasn't exactly a sport but it was sports-related. And Kurt was on the cross-country team; so what was wrong with sports?

Sports were fun, healthy, and profitable too. A number of Glendale's seniors had received athletic scholarships to top-rated colleges last year. They had all been guys. It could still happen to her someday. Female athletics were catching on in most colleges, like UCLA, Old Dominion, and Notre Dame. They were all putting big money into their female sports programs. As for her social life, what about Beth and Sheila? She knew they weren't guys. But she didn't need guys. Guys were all right, but they wanted to monopolize your time, and she had things to do.

"Forget it, mom. I'm still not going to have a lot of time for making new friends."

Placing the duck back into the oven to keep it warm, Mrs. Vickers heard a sigh. She walked toward the butcher block table and sat down. Caroline sat down next to her and waited.

"Why won't you have time, Caroline?" her mother asked.

"Basketball tryouts begin in a week, mom, and since I was on the team last year, I'm a shoo-in this year."

"Oh, Caroline. I thought you said you weren't going to play basketball this year. You said if you tried out for the hockey squad and made it, you'd pass up basketball."

"I know I did, mom. But I changed my mind. I had fun playing hockey; but I love basketball. I want to play this year, too."

"But your grades . . ."

"My grades are all right. I'm not failing anything. I'm a B/C student, for goodness sake."

"But you could do so much better if you had more time to study. And when was the last time you went out on a date? Last summer? You haven't been to a school dance all year. Do you plan on going to the Sadie Hawkins Dance at least?" Mrs. Vickers asked.

Caroline knew what her mother was after. It was just her round-about way of trying to find out if Caroline were interested in anyone, or if someone were interested in her. She knew what her mother wanted to hear but . . .

"I don't know," she sighed. "How did you know about that anyway?"

"It's an annual event, Caroline, that takes place the same time each year. I remember your sister getting anxious about this time every year," she reminisced. "She was always afraid someone would ask the boy she wanted to go with before she got a chance."

Darn Bobbie anyway, thought Caroline. She was Miss Popularity in school. All the cheerleaders were, according to her older sister. Well, she was different. Her interests were different. I'm not going to live my high school career like Bobbie, she promised herself. No way. That's just not me.

Seeing Caroline's determined expression, Mrs. Vickers grasped her hand, lightly drawing her daughter's eyes toward her own.

"I just want you to be happy," she said.

"But I am, mom. I don't mind not dating— much. I don't have the time anyway," she added, laughing.

Her mother did not join in with Caroline's laughter. Instead she slowly rose and said, "Then maybe you'd better organize your schedule to make time for that—and your grades, too."

Before she could reply, loud barking and

male voices echoed from the foyer. It was her father and brother.

"I'll go wash up now," Caroline said quickly. It was a chicken's way out, but she had had enough for one evening. All she wanted was Amber and the safety of her room.

2

The school cafeteria was filled with talkative students by the time Caroline got out of her American History class. She and several other students were asked to remain behind to discuss their term-paper topics. Caroline's choice—The Pinkerton Detective Agency and Its Role in the Investigation of Abraham Lincoln's Death—was well received by Mr. Camp, a new teacher at Glendale—fresh out of college and full of innovative ideas for his classes.

Her topic wasn't an easy one and would

need a lot of research, she knew. But Mr. Camp had said hers was one of the more interesting topics submitted. He even suggested several books. Now with the additional two titles Mr. Camp had given her, she knew she'd have enough information to write a reasonably good paper—*if* she started it before basketball practice began. Oh the perils of team sports! Caroline had already let too much time pass without working on the assignment at all.

Scanning the sea of smiling and laughing faces, Caroline sought out her friends while sidestepping the more preoccupied students, busily balancing heavily laden trays.

Ugghhh . . . mystery meat! Again Caroline was glad she took the time to pack a lunch every morning. She was sure cafeteria food wasn't even good enough to cross Amber's sensitive palate, let alone her own. Good old liverwurst on whole wheat with mayo and lots of onions would do just nicely, thank you.

The din of talking students was even louder today than usual. But after all it *was* "Mad Monday." The weekend was over so everyone had to catch up on the latest weekend happenings—who went out with whom; where they went, what she wore, etc., etc. Boring. Boring. Boring. Right? Wrong, thought Caroline as she chastized herself. Be honest. It wouldn't be boring if it were you. You'd like to come in here on Monday and have a tale or two to tell about Matt Anderson.

It was strange. Caroline had barely spoken a complete sentence to him her entire time at Glendale; yet all her fantasies these days centered around Matt. She first noticed him last year during one of Glendale's first football games. He was a good player and popular among the fans. Like just about every other freshman girl, Caroline developed a crush on him. It amounted to nothing, as she knew it would, but still she never quite got over those "puppy love" feelings. Caroline would see him at other sports events or occasionally in the hallway, and inevitably she'd wonder what it would be like to be his girl.

I wonder how Matt spends his weekends, she mused. He's probably busy beating the girls back with a stick. A smile crossed her lips as she imagined the brawny grid star fending off diminutive females with a baseball bat. It was so funny she almost broke out laughing.

"Hey, Slim! Smiling to yourself again? You know they put people away for that, don't you?"

Caroline's face was an open book. Too often her inner thoughts were mirrored upon it. And just as frequently she paid the consequences. Like now.

Glancing in the direction of the needling

voice, Caroline saw Beth and Sheila beckoning her to their table. It was Sheila who continued the razzing. Pointing theatrically into the distance she exclaimed, "Oh, look. The men in white coats are coming to take her away." In unison all heads swiveled toward a far corner of the cafeteria, only to see two soda vendors struggling with large metal tanks in order to refill the soda machines.

Caroline could feel her cheeks flush red. "Okay, okay, you two. Give me a break. Heaven knows, if anyone is going to be taken anywhere it's going to be you turkeys," she said crisply to her two friends.

Beth looked stunned and silence fell over the table at Caroline's outburst. But she couldn't hold the moment for long. No matter how she tried, she couldn't control her facial muscles; in no time a lopsided smile broke through.

"I hate it when you do that," Beth shouted. "I never know when you're really angry or just kidding."

"Serves you right, Adams," Caroline replied and the three friends laughed good-naturedly as room was made for her at the table.

Adams, Richardson, and Vickers. They were the three stooges. The three musketeers —rather "mouseketeers" ever since that Halloween when they'd dressed up as Mickey, Minnie, and Milly Mouse. Technically, Mickey and Minnie had never been married and never had "a little rat—uhh, brat," Beth had joked at the time. But they wanted to go to their fourth-grade party as a group—so poetic license, of sorts, was taken.

The three girls had been together since their first days at Spring Garden Elementary School. When they graduated to the Middle School luck stayed with them. They were in the same grade section. Even now, though the alphabetical system placed them in different homerooms, they managed to schedule some classes together. Normally, only two of them were in the same class at a time. This year, however, they had lucked out again. The three of them were starting the year in three classes together—gym, biology, and English. Gym, of course, was *the* best since it gave them the chance to goof off and catch up on the day's happenings.

The passing years had cemented their friendship. They went through the trauma of braces and first dates together. Who cared if Caroline's was a blind date set up by Sheila? They were like sisters. "Better than sisters," Caroline often remarked, since she and her sister, Bobbie, had never really gotten along. Naturally, they all hoped they'd be going off to college together in a couple of years. But though she wished they *could* remain together, Caroline was more realistic. Athletics

were very important to Caroline and she'd go
to any college with a good women's athletic
program. She wanted to attend one of the
best, like UCLA, USC, or Old Dominion—and
on an athletic scholarship to boot. She was
reaching for the top but her mind was set. She
could be the next Carol "Blaze" Blazejowski,
Anne Meyers, or Nancy Lieberman. She'd win
the NCAA's National Women's Collegiate
Basketball Championship. In a few years she
could be filming TV commercials with a big
NBA basketball player or narrating a CBS
Sports Spectacular. The opportunities were
endless and she knew she had the talent. And
she was ready to spend time practicing to
refine it. She was a firm believer that if a
person worked hard enough success would
follow. In that respect Caroline was like her
father, the eternal and ever-present optimist
in her life. He was always giving her that
extra push to try and try again. When she was
a child their favorite story was *The Little
Train That Could.* It was the first book she
ever learned to read straight through, and
when times got rough she remembered its
simple moral . . . *keep trying and never give
up*.

Caroline was starving by the time she set
her lunch before her. She hadn't had time for
breakfast this morning. Hungrily, she dove in

and was too busy munching on Sheila's fritos to pay attention to any of the conversations going on at the table. However, Beth's voice finally caught her ear.

"You know," Beth sighed. "I still can't believe field hockey season is over. Want my extra cupcake, Slim?"

"Was that all one sentence or two?" Caroline asked teasingly. Beth didn't bother to reply. She just stuck out her tongue.

"Thanks anyway," Caroline continued with a negative shake of her head, "but I'll just eat my sandwich. Cupcakes are *fat-ten-ning*," she emphasized.

"I know," Beth replied. "But I *need* to put on a *little* weight. I ran myself ragged those last couple of games backing you up. Not to mention the hours of sleep I lost toward the end of the season because I was too nervous to sleep. All of that can really take a toll on a girl's figure."

"Okay, Beth. You made your point," Caroline said with a smile.

At five feet two inches Beth wasn't much taller than she had been in elementary school. She had the petite stature that attracted guys. "It brings out their protective nature," she had said more than once with that slow exaggerated wink that made her look as if she had something in her eye.

And who could ignore Sheila? The entire male population was in love with her sea blue eyes and strawberry blonde hair. Her hair was an eyecatcher all right, baby fine and natural, it seemed to have a life of its own. Less than friendly females kept the rumor alive that her locks were courtesy of Miss Clairol. But there were a few lucky males that after a closer look were only to happy to set the record straight. There wasn't a dark root in sight. Her sparkling girl-next-door good looks definitely made her the glamour girl of the trio, which would have broken up many a friendship. But Sheila never played up to it which set her apart from some of the so-called "glamour girls" at Glendale.

Absentmindedly Caroline picked the crust off her liverwurst sandwich as she computed her own assets. Tall, nice eyes and hair, so mom says.

I'm not exactly a bow-wow myself, she thought, but Sheila does have more than her share of male attention. Then again she works at it, though she doesn't flaunt it. She always wears nail polish and knows just what styles are in. I guess it all depends on what a person's priorities are. Looking together and boys are Sheila's, and sports are mine. And that's that. But can't a girl have both?

"Oh, look what you've done!"

Jolted from her thoughts, Caroline glanced down the length of the table in time to see Lucy Allen simultaneously chastizing a red-faced student and frantically mopping a Coke spill on her blouse. Lucy was intelligent and well spoken but a snob by Caroline's standards. She was attractive and she knew it. If you didn't hang out with the "right crowd" you didn't exist in her book. She was also one of the senior cheerleaders and one of the more popular girls at Glendale High.

"I'll be right back," Sheila announced. "Lucy can use my glass of water to clean the stain."

"You're a saint, Richardson. I wouldn't even waste my time," Caroline said.

"Now, Slim—Lucy's not bad. You might like her if you gave her a chance," Sheila replied.

"If I gave *her* a chance—who ignores whom around here anyway?" Caroline complained. "If you're not a cheerleader or a guy she looks right through you."

Hesitating, Sheila looked as if she wanted to say something more, but instead picked up her glass and walked away. Caroline turned her full attention on Beth and with her characteristic burst of enthusiasm began chattering away.

"Do you realize that tryouts for basketball begin next week? That means the season opener is just around the corner! Isn't that great? I told my mother I was going to play ball again this year. She was a little upset. But how could I break up the gang? I can't wait for the season to start."

Caught up in her own excitement, Caroline failed to notice the downward glances of Beth and Sheila, who had returned in time to hear her comment. When silence answered her talkative outburst, Caroline realized something was wrong. Her friends appeared to be extraordinarily absorbed with cleaning their nails and collecting the table trash.

"Hey. What is it? Aren't you looking forward to basketball?"

The continued silence was agonizing as she waited for one of them to speak. It was Sheila's misfortune to finish her nails before Beth was through with the trash. When Caroline got eye contact she wouldn't let go. There was nothing left for Sheila to do but clear her throat and plunge right in.

"Well, Carrie, Beth and I have been talking. We just barely made the freshman squad last year because only a few went out for the team. And we didn't get asked to play on the junior varsity squad the way you did."

"But *we* did play on the freshman squad together," Caroline interrupted. "We were a team. We *are* a team. You guys are sure to make the JV squad this year. All the seniors from last year's Varsity squad are gone, so everyone is bound to move up. You'll make the JV squad with no problem and the three of us will be together."

Faced with Caroline's determination and pleading expression, Sheila played with her hair, a habit of hers whenever she was nervous. By now Beth had finished placing the trash in a neat little pile of folded grease-stained paper bags. She sat on her chair with a trapped look on her face.

"Well *you're* quiet," Caroline said to her meaningfully. "Don't just sit there like a bump on a log. Say something!"

"Oh, Carrie, don't be angry. Let's face it. You're a better athlete than we are. You're more dedicated than we are."

A sinking feeling began to fill Caroline's stomach. She knew what was coming and wished she could do something to prevent it.

"Caroline," Sheila began calmly, "even if *I did* make the team, I'd want to quit before too long because my heart wouldn't be in it. There are really other things I'd like to try before I have to kiss good old Glendale goodbye and there are other things that Beth would like to try, too."

"Like what?" Caroline asked. She wasn't going to make this easy for them.

"Well, I think I'd like to try out for the Glee Club," Beth chimed in. "I've got a pretty good voice. You've said that yourself, Carrie."

My mistake, Caroline thought.

"Also it will give me more time to study. I got the word from the folks. If I don't get my grades up, I can start looking for another home. Do you believe it? Everyone's trying to stop the 'runaway' problem and *my* parents are willing to contribute to it."

Beth's attempt to lessen the tension surrounding the threesome was lost on Caroline, yet she was surprised at how calm she felt. "And what about you?" she said, turning to Sheila. "What do you think you'd like to do?"

"I want to try out for the Christmas play," she said hurriedly.

A smile found its way to Caroline's lips for the first time since their conversation began. There was plenty of time before auditions for the Christmas play. Sheila could play basketball now and audition later if she still wanted to. By that time Caroline was sure that she'd forget the whole thing. Then at least she wouldn't be deserted by Sheila.

"For Pete's sake, Sheila, auditions have got to be at least a month away, and . . ."

"And," Sheila interjected, "I want to join the cheerleading squad. A couple of girls were booted from the squad," she added quickly, "because of 'undignified behavior' after the last football game. You know—'ambassadors abroad,' 'representatives of the school' and all that. They were caught . . .”

“Okay. I get the drift. It looks like that 'old gang of mine' is breaking up. It had to happen sometime. Deep down inside I think we all knew that. I just didn't think it would be so soon.”

“Oh, Caroline, don't be hurt,” Beth implored. “We'll still be in classes together.”

“I know,” Caroline replied. She felt she had to get away from the table for a while. “I'm going to get another soda before the bell rings. I'm dying of thirst.” She rummaged through her purse, scattering part of its contents on the table as she gathered the necessary coins. “I'll be right back.”

Walking across the cafeteria, Caroline couldn't believe what had happened. What a bummer, she thought. This day can't get any worse. Now I know how Julius Caesar felt when Brutus and the boys got finished with him.

The row of soda and candy machines was relatively vacant. She slipped the change into an unoccupied machine and pressed her selection. No Tab for me. I definitely need a Pepsi.

Flipping the lid open, she leaned against the machine and took a long, slow drink. Casually observing her fellow classmates, she smiled to some and briefly chatted with others although she didn't really feel like it. Life was certainly full of surprises.

While taking a sip of her drink a tall figure caught her eye. Matt Anderson, she mused. He's a junior. This isn't his lunch period. What's he doing in here? It *could* be his free period. But still, he's not supposed to be in here now.

Question after question entered her mind as she stared at the distant figure. She was so preoccupied she was surprised to find Beth standing beside her.

"Just came over to see what happened to you. That's Matt Anderson over there, isn't it?"

"Uh huh."

"Used to see him running with the football team when they had to do their laps near our hockey field. He returned a few balls that got past you, didn't he?"

"Uh huh."

Exasperated at her pal's lack of response, Beth chided her. "Earth to Caroline. Earth to Caroline. Come in, please."

Lowering her head quickly, Caroline turned and spoke softly to her persistent friend.

"He's smiling at me, Beth. Can you believe it?"

"Yes," she replied too casually. "Yes, I can

believe it. The *question* is can you believe he's walking over here?"

"You're kidding. He's not."

"No, I'm not, kiddo. See—you—later—Slim," she said slyly, leaving Caroline standing all alone.

Caroline felt like an idiot standing there with an empty soda can in her hand. But she was afraid to move. Maybe Beth was kidding and he wasn't coming over but she didn't want to peer over and find out. She'd look too eager and even though she was, she didn't want him to know it. Yet, she was afraid to walk away as well. If he were coming over, he might take it as a brush off. But who in her right mind would do that to him? As she pondered that question, a deep, resonant voice said hello.

"Hi," she replied shyly.

"Caroline Vickers, right?"

"Matt Anderson, right?"

They both laughed briefly, shattering the charged atmosphere that seemed to surround them. Caroline felt as though there weren't enough air to breathe.

She couldn't get over how tall Matt was! It was a novelty to be looking up at a guy. Looking down on guys always made her feel like a giant. If they were her height it was okay. But if they were taller it was the best of all.

"I've seen you practice hockey a couple a times," he said. I even watched a couple of your home games while I was supposed to be working out."

"I hope you didn't get into trouble."

"No—the coach is strict but he's a real pussycat at heart."

Their laughter flowed easier now, as they relaxed a little. Caroline was fascinated by his blue eyes. They were even bluer than Sheila's and that was quite a feat. They were shocking in contrast to his black curly hair and the combination reminded Caroline of an artist's rendering of Napoleon Bonaparte. Did Napoleon have blue eyes? She couldn't remember. Not that it mattered. She'd rather be there talking with Matt then playing Josephine to a short Napoleon, an amusing thought which made her smile broadly.

"Well," he began awkwardly. "I have to go. I was delivering a message to one of the proctors. I just wanted to stop and congratulate you on the team's winning season. My older sister used to play on the team a few years back. She's a sophomore in college now. She suffered through a couple of losing seasons on the hockey team. She'll go wild when I tell her how well you—I mean the team—did."

"Thanks," said Caroline. Darn it, why can't

I think of anything else to say. He'll think I'm a bore, she reproved herself.

"Sure . . ." he said awkwardly, before turning to stride off. Her heart skipped a beat as he veered around suddenly and came up to her again. "Caroline . . . I know you don't know me that well . . . But would you like to go out for a Coke or something after school? I could pick you up at your homeroom after last period . . . if you would tell me where that is."

"Room 202," she said faintly. Could she have heard Matt correctly? Was he really asking her for a date?

"Great," he said, smiling broadly. He broke into a brisk jog and had disappeared into the passing throng before she could say another word.

The bell rang and Caroline barely heard it. She was beside herself with happiness and practically ran back to the table to collect her things.

He asked me out, she said over and over to herself. *He actually asked me out.* Do you believe it?

As planned, Matt picked Caroline up at her homeroom at the end of the day. They decided to go to Friendly's. It was *the* popular place to be since the Buchanan Soda Shop had closed.

As they searched for an open booth many

waves and greetings were tossed their way. Sheila was there with Lucy Allen and one or two other cheerleaders. Lucy looked as though she were holding court. Caroline was pleased to note a look of surprise on all their faces when she and Matt walked by. She hadn't discussed their "date" with Sheila or Beth when she returned to the lunch table. Both her friends had seen them talking together and had tried pumping Caroline for details. But Caroline had been noncommittal and suddenly remembered she had to talk to an instructor before the period began. She had hastily bid her friends so long but not before seeing the questioning and hurt glances they exchanged. They had been surprised by her secretive attitude, quite a switch from her talkativeness in the past, especially whenever Matt had been the subject. Caroline knew it had been a childish way to get even with her friends, but she hadn't cared. They were removing themselves from her life, so she had the right to do the same.

Thinking back on her actions Caroline felt confused. Maybe she had been wrong. All she was sure of at the moment was that she wasn't going to spoil her good time thinking about that. *She was with Matt Anderson.* How often had she dreamed of being with him like this with the eyes of some of the popular doers and shakers of Glendale High upon them! Later, she'd think about Beth and Sheila, but not now.

Caroline had never realized just how popular Matt was. Many of his friends gestured for him to join them and Caroline was pleased when he declined their offers. He obviously wanted her all to himself and she felt pleasantly flushed when he touched her shoulder and steered her toward a vacant booth against a side wall.

Cokes, french fries, and cheeseburgers were ordered in no time from a passing waitress who was only too happy to wait on Matt. To Matt's credit he acted as if he didn't notice the extra attention. Two points in his favor. If there was anything Caroline hated, it was conceit. It was after they had ordered their snack that Matt had said her hair smelled terrific. It was a comment made so totally out of the blue and sounding so much like a TV commercial too that Caroline couldn't control a small outburst of laughter. Matt blushed, but quickly bounced back and told a funny anecdote about his freshman year tryout for the football squad. Soon they were both laughing comfortably. They spent the next half-hour sharing their lives and those of their families.

Caroline learned that Matt was the eldest of

three boys in a family of four. His older sister, Sherry, graduated from Glendale the same year as her sister, Bobbi, had. Now Sherry was a junior at the University of Pennsylvania studying business administration. She had been captain of the hockey team her junior and senior years in high school and had been somewhat of a star to boot—even though the Chargers never had a winning season.

Between mouthfuls of cheeseburger and french fries, Caroline attempted to tell him of her family tree, but Matt wouldn't let her get a word in edgewise. He knew every member of her family in one way or another. He used to run into Caroline's brother in the men's locker room since Kurt was a member of the fall cross-country team. He knew of her sister Bobbi through his own sister. And her parents were upstanding members of the community and were active on several town committees that his own mother and father were on.

"Let's face it, Caroline," he said when he was through giving his rundown of the Vickers clan. "You're the only Vickers I don't know." Then he had taken his napkin and wiped some errant ketchup from her chin. Caroline was a little embarrassed by her sloppiness but Matt's next words made her quickly forget her clumsiness.

"Yeah," he continued in a low, modulated

tone. "You're the only Vickers I don't know—
but the one I'd like to know most."

Caroline was flabbergasted. Although she
was enjoying the afternoon she had been holding her breath the entire time, hoping she
wouldn't say or do something stupid, hoping
Matt would like her. But not in her wildest
dreams had she expected this! She had never
expected such a direct declaration of—interest. He had caught her completely off guard
and she didn't know what to say. All she knew
was that she'd better say something fast for
Matt was waiting. It was Matt who filled the
silence.

"Well, don't keep me in suspense," he
chuckled. "After that little bombshell you
must have something you want to say even if
it's—slow down pardner," he drawled in a
western accent.

To her surprise, Caroline saw his lips part
in a tremulous half smile. Why he's just as
nervous as I am, she thought.

She had been so busy thinking about herself
that she only now had really looked at him. He
has as much at stake as I do. Maybe even
more since he does the asking, she told herself. "I'm glad it's not just me," she said
aloud.

Matt's quizzical expression brought laughter to her lips.

"I beg your pardon?" he said.

"I like you too—pardner," she drawled.

"Terrific!" he bellowed, drawing some amused glances from the tenants of neighboring booths. "Now how about a strawberry milkshake for dessert?"

3

Caroline couldn't remember the last time she had had so much fun—with a guy, that was. Yes, she, Beth, and Sheila had done a lot together—horseback riding, rollerskating, bowling and the like. They had shared a snack or two at Friendly's but it wasn't the same. Being with Matt was different. He made Caroline feel small and feminine for the first time, and she loved it!

The days following their initial get together passed all too rapidly for Caroline. There were mundane tasks to perform and Caroline continued to do her share of laundry, dishes, and grocery shopping. She even convinced her mother she needed a new winter coat and spent an hour or so one evening window shopping. There was still time for Matt in the evening too. It was so easy. Without a hockey practice or game to rush off to after classes there was time to do everything and Caroline thoroughly enjoyed her new-found freedom.

Sometimes Matt would pick her up at her homeroom and they'd return to Friendly's for a snack, leaving Caroline to pick over her dinner later once she got home. Or perhaps after spending a couple of hours at the library writing her paper, Matt would pick her up and take her for a drive along the scenic Glendale streets.

One of the oldest and more historical communities in the area, Glendale had several huge mansions on prestigious Highland Heights and boasted of a variety of unique architectural forms dating back to the American Revolution. Over crackling, dry leaves they would drive slowly by the gracious old homes with their sloping lawns and ancient trees.

Their relationship was now upbeat and easy. They enjoyed each other's company and never lacked for something to talk about. But Caroline had one quirk. She never let Matt park in front of her home, nor did she let him walk her to the front door. It was part of the "dating" ritual that was absent in their relationship. If Matt noticed, he didn't let on. Or possibly Caroline's variety of excuses were not as transparent as she thought. It was either too cold or drizzly for Matt to bother to get out of the car and take that short walk to her door. Or else Caroline would ask to be dropped off at the library, so she could do some research for one of her classes.

To Caroline the lies were necessary but she never failed to feel guilty afterward. She knew it was wrong to lie to Matt and his honesty and gentleness with her only made her deception that much worse.

Caroline wanted to keep her friendship with Matt a secret. Her reasons for her behavior were many, but the focal point was her mother. Ever since Caroline told her mother of her plans to play basketball, things had been tense between them. Mrs. Vickers just wouldn't accept the fact Caroline wanted to play basketball. And when Mrs. Vickers ran into Sheila's mother and discovered Sheila was trying out for the cheerleading squad, she hinted that Caroline should do the same.

"Think of all the nice girls you'll get to know," Mrs. Vickers had said. "And remember, cheerleaders *are* the most popular girls in high school. Think of all the boys you'll meet."

Caroline wouldn't give in. She wanted to play basketball and saw no reason why she shouldn't. Even if her mother weren't crazy about the idea, her father was all for it which ended any serious discussion on the matter.

It was difficult for Caroline but she could have made life easier for herself by telling her mother about Matt. It would have made her mother happy and given her something to boast about at the next gathering of her friends. It also would have given Caroline a little peace, but now Caroline saw it as a matter of principle.

She didn't want her mother to think she was seeing Matt to please her or to be one of *the crowd* at school. She was seeing Matt because she liked him and he liked her. She and Matt had found each other and she wanted him all to herself for a while until she was really sure of his feelings for her and until her mother was ready to accept her as she was.

Even Beth and Sheila were kept in the dark about Matt, which was a much harder task for Caroline. The threesome had been through so much together. Caroline's blossoming relationship with Matt should have been the cause for celebration and friendly teasing. But her friends' decision to pursue other activities was a blow that Caroline hadn't recovered from. She took it personally and in her hurt she wanted to hurt them too. Only through her silence about herself and Matt could she do this.

This isn't to say that Caroline had hidden her friendship with Matt. She couldn't have, even had she wanted to. They were already the hottest item of gossip at Glendale. Caroline just didn't volunteer any information to her friends about them. In fact she kept her contact with her friends to a minimum. Instead of sitting next to her friends in class, Caroline's late arrival insured that all the choice seats in the back would be taken and she would be "forced" to sit up front. Of if she happened to arrive in time to sit next to one of her friends and exchange a few pleasantries, she always hurried out of the class afterward. She behaved the same way over lunch hour and she knew her friends were aware of her attitude and probably puzzled and hurt.

It was quite a week for Caroline, one of beginnings and possible endings. But Caroline was just too involved in the former with Matt to think about Beth and Sheila at all.

Caroline's carefree days of fun with Matt passed quickly. The weekend was just a blur of memories, and before she knew it a new busy week had begun. Moments not spent daydreaming about Matt were spent on homework assignments and basketball tryouts. And after a few days, Caroline again found herself playing catch up when it came to her homework. It was a wonder she got the grades she did. Grades just weren't that important to her. There was only one arena in which she excelled and felt confident—sports. For Caroline, homework was just something to be worked in—somehow.

Of all the sports she played, basketball was her favorite. Basketball was to her what ballet must be to Baryshnikov or tennis to Chris Everett Lloyd. Playing basketball and playing it well gave her a feeling of accomplishment, and after a long exhausting workout there was nothing like a hot, steaming shower. It was a fitting end to a hard session and a very busy week.

Actually, after Friday's tryout Caroline would really have loved to take a leisurely soak in the whirlpool, but the girls' locker room at Glendale didn't have one, and only in special situations could they use the boys'. That area was strictly off limits to all females. Even the women gym instructors and coaches couldn't enter unescorted. Only when absolutely needed were those hallowed halls opened to female athletes in need of special therapy, properly supervised of course. It was the old double standard as far as Caroline was concerned and a discriminatory practice she hoped not to face in college.

Adjusting the shower temperature to as hot as she could stand it, Caroline cautiously stepped into its cascading spray. As the water pelted her body and the steam rose to engulf her, Caroline began to relax. She felt like standing there forever but showers were at a premium right then. When more of the girls finished their laps around the basketball court, the locker room would be a madhouse of females trying to get into a shower before everyone else. Caroline was just lucky that she and only one or two others had finished their laps first. She was quick enough to get her favorite shower too—first row left, in the back, right near the heat ventilation system. Reaching for the baby shampoo she had left on the wooden bench on the other side of the shower curtain, she started to wash her shoulder-length, slightly wavy hair. She couldn't wait to wash it again. She had always been a fanatic about having clean hair.

Working up a good head of lather, she briskly scrubbed her scalp until it tingled. She was content and relaxed, so relaxed that her mind began to drift. Boy, was she glad it was Friday, the last day of a very long week. But more than that it was the last day of tryouts. In her mind, *her* first week of the basketball season was over. She had never considered the possibility of failure. The list of this year's Varsity and JV Squads would be posted before she left the locker room that evening; she was sure her name would be on it.

Overall Caroline was pleased with her performance this past week. She had really enjoyed the competition and camaraderie of the girls who tried out.

The physical exertion of the warm-up exercises, laps, drills, and scrimmages were stimulating. Sure, her muscles ached a little, but not as badly as most of the girls', she could tell. The field hockey season had prepared her. She was still in good physical condition. It was just the sadness and feeling of loneliness touching her when she least expected it that bothered her.

Some girls from last year's teams had been out again this year. Coach Cooper (M.C. to the girls) was still the basketball coach. But true to their words, Sheila and Beth didn't try out and Caroline missed them. She didn't even have Matt's company to look forward to, for with the beginning of the week's tryouts she just hadn't had time to see him, except for chance meetings in the hallways.

Sighing, Caroline began rinsing the shampoo from her hair. Some of it entered her eyes diverting her from her unpleasant thoughts.

"Darn it, where's my towel," she groaned.

Hastily Caroline groped about for it, wetting her designer jeans and aqua blue velour crew-

neck sweater as she did so. Only after stub-
bing her toe and nearly falling out of the
shower did she find it. On the floor, naturally.
And if that weren't enough, she suddenly felt
as if she were standing in a wind tunnel. The
outer curtain was pulled back, and poking her
head into the stall was Valerie Davis.

Caroline really liked Valerie. As a junior
transfer student from a private high school in
Connecticut, she came to Glendale not knowing anyone but had quickly made friends.
Caroline and she had been paired during a
number of drills and Caroline hoped she had
made the team. Valerie was her type of person
—a real team player.

"Ooops, sorry, Carrie," the older girl said.
"I thought this one was up for grabs. You
wouldn't be getting out now, would you?"

"No, not quite yet. I was just getting some
shampoo out of my eyes," she replied, squint-
ing in Valerie's general direction.

"Okay. Sorry to intrude. Oh—by the way, I
think M.C. is looking for you," Valerie said as
she left.

Stepping back into the shower, Caroline
finished the job of rinsing her hair. Now girls
were filing into the locker room. Caroline
could hear their chatter even above the sound
of her shower. Caroline loved the sound a
running shower made. It reminded her of a
thunderstorm or a summer shower depending

upon the intensity of the spray. The sound of
rain always gave her a peaceful feeling. It
slowed down her inner think track; just like
the shower was doing now, as she massaged
her scalp, mindless of the female hordes clam-
oring for a vacant shower stall. Just as she
felt herself drifting into pleasant oblivion it
hit her. M.C. wants to see me. The list must be
up by now and she usually likes to see those
girls she's passed over as soon as possible
after the list is posted. Oh no! She couldn't
have cut me!

Caroline must have broken some kind of
speed record for getting dressed. She was in
such a hurry that she didn't bother to blow dry
her hair. She merely towel dried it as best she
could.

As she moved toward the main bulletin
board where the lists were indeed posted, the
faces of her fellow athletes told their story all
too well. After reading the lists, many who
hadn't made the team quickly collected their
belongings and left. There were also a few
others who after "trying to reason" with the
coach stood around and complained, adding
to the general confusion of the moment. Most,
however, accepted the decision in true sports-
woman fashion. Caroline was glad. She
couldn't cope with tears and felt useless in the
face of someone else's unhappiness. She

never knew what to say at such a time. She only knew how she would feel if in their shoes.

Standing in front of the bulletin board, Caroline frantically searched for her name on the JV roster. Had she missed it in her haste? She read it again. A lump formed in the back of her throat. Her body sagged and went completely cold. Her name was simply not there.

With head bowed and fists clenched, Caroline felt her eyes misting. I will not cry. Not here. Not with everyone around.

"You got cut too, huh?" a disgruntled voice said, disrupting her thoughts. "She's some coach. I guess if we had played up to her, our names would be on that list too."

Despite her own grief and disappointment Caroline knew that statement was unfair. Coach Cooper was a good coach who didn't play favorites. And she wasn't going to stand by and let a sore loser talk about her like that. Turning toward the complaining athlete, Caroline gave her a withering stare. It was obviously not the response that Caroline's companion expected and in seconds Caroline stood alone.

Once more Caroline turned to the board before moving away. She glanced idly at the Varsity listing. *There it was. Her name* near the bottom on the list. Althea Wallace held last place honors this time. Darn this school and its alphabetical listing! What a relief! What a surprise! She had never considered the possibility of making the Varsity Squad! Oh, if only Beth and Sheila were here! Again Caroline felt a longing for her friends but she shook it off as she would have a leg cramp.

Valerie Davis came up to her, offering congratulations. Caroline was pleased to discover Valerie had made the team too. Elated beyond words, Caroline approached the coach's office with a light step. Confidently, she rapped on the open door and briskly entered.

A chunky five feet three with pepper hair and almond-colored eyes, M.C. Cooper was not what many expected a basketball coach to look like. But she was good. Her quick wit, knowledge of the game, and fairness made her very popular with her teams and her gym classes too. At her age (no one knew for sure what that was) she could still go a few court lengths with the best of them. She was a great teacher, and Caroline had learned a lot from her the year before.

"Well, here you are at last," the coach began as she swiveled her chair around to face Caroline. "I take it you've seen the bulletin board?"

"Yes," Caroline stammered, moving towels and gym gear from the only chair available.

She sat down. "I just want to thank you for putting me on the Varsity team. I never dreamed . . ."

"Woa, woa," her coach interjected. "*I* didn't put you on anything. *You* put yourself on the Varsity team. You worked hard, showed a lot of enthusiasm and improved a great deal in the past year. The other girls like you too and I know you'll work well with them." She smiled. "I have to admit though, I heard some talk earlier in the year that you weren't coming out for the team this year. I don't know if that was a serious consideration of yours or not. I'm glad you changed your mind."

What could Caroline say to that? A high school was a little world unto itself and the Glendale "grapevine" was notorious. Students found out they failed or passed tests before they even saw their scores. So why should she be surprised?

"I have to admit I was thinking about not coming out again. I thought field hockey and tennis would be enough for me, but the closer it came to basketball season the more excited I got. I just knew I had to play again. Please don't think I was thinking about not coming out because of you."

A blush quickly spread across Caroline's face. She didn't mean that the way it sounded.

"What I mean is, you had nothing to do with

my decision to come out for basketball." Good grief. I'm making it worse. Caroline bit her lips before she embarrassed herself further.

Barely stifling her laughter, Coach Cooper leaned forward and patted Caroline's hand. "I know what you're trying to say, Carrie. I'm just happy you worked things out."

Withdrawing her hand, Coach Cooper sat back and settled her frame in a more comfortable position. "But as to the reason I asked you here."

Imperceptibly Caroline tensed. Surely this was no reason for alarm. She was on the team; so what could be wrong?

"It's your grades, Caroline," Coach Cooper said. "As you know it's the school's policy, and a good one I might add, to check the grades of all potential athletes for any of Glendale's competitive teams. Unfortunately, I had to cut a couple of girls from the team today simply because they were failing a course. According to your geometry teacher you're not doing that well. You're a C minus or D student who's just barely hanging on by the skin of your teeth. But Mr. Jeffers is confident you could do better if you'd just put more of an effort into your studies. The next few weeks will be hectic and, remember, the basketball season does last longer than field hockey's. I'd hate to have to drop you from the team halfway through the season, but if you start failing geometry I'll have no choice. Mr. Jeffers said you failed a quiz a week or two ago."

"But it didn't count," Caroline said quickly.

"I know it didn't. Mr. Jeffers told me that too. I felt I had to broach the subject with you and put all my cards on the table. Sports aren't more important than your grades, Caroline. They're merely the icing on the cake that make high school and life more interesting. In the long run your grades are more important. They'll have more of an impact on your future than sports will. I hope you remember that."

Caroline's remaining talk with the coach was brief. M.C. had big plans for this year's teams and the returning players were the key. Caroline promised to work hard on her geometry and although the interview ended on a good note, she still felt like she had just fouled out of a game. A warning had been given and she couldn't ignore it.

How can M.C. say sports aren't important? Maybe it isn't for some of the other girls but it is to me! If Mr. Jeffers wasn't such a hard marker I'd have a solid C by now. Maybe even a B. Why can't some people mind their own business, she thought bitterly as she hurried to meet Valerie.

It was close to seven at night by the time Caroline got home. Her little get-together with Valerie had been fun and really gave her flagging spirits a needed lift after her talk with M.C. By the time she entered her home she couldn't wait to tell everyone her good news.

"I'm home," she yelled happily, only to be greeted by a stern, "Will you keep it down, I'm on the phone," from her brother.

I made Varsity, she silently mouthed to him. A broad grin appeared on Kurt's face as he ecstatically gave her the thumbs up sign.

Crossing the landing Caroline entered the living room to find both her parents dressed for an evening out. Although married for almost twenty years, her parents still believed in keeping the romance in their relationship. One night a week was *their* night; tonight was obviously it.

Her father looked handsome in his navy blue suit. His light brown hair was moderately long now but he wore the extra length well. He was even wearing the tie she'd given him for Christmas. Scooping up Amber who had skidded into the room upon hearing her arrival, she walked over to her father who was standing by the fireplace and kissed his cheek. She was almost as tall as he was but he still had to lean over slightly to kiss his youngest in return.

"Going out to dinner, I see," she said jovially.

"Yes—we're having a little night out on the town," he said in his best W.C. Fields voice. "Dinner and the movies. How's that for a couple of old folks."

"Speak for yourself, Ted," her mother said briskly.

She had been sitting in her husband's favorite leather chair sipping a glass of sherry. It was their little ritual before they went out and tonight was no exception. Mrs. Vickers looked slim and pretty in her beige cashmere dress. It was hard for Caroline to think of her parents as old. They were both well built and very attractive people. Most times they acted like newlyweds instead of "old marrieds."

Well—there was no time like the present. Taking a deep breath, Caroline stayed by her father's side for moral support and announced her good news.

"Guess what? Basketball tryouts ended today. The teams have been selected. I made the Varsity Squad."

"Why, honey," Mr. Vickers said, drawing her close, "that's terrific!" Inwardly Caroline thanked her father. She could always count on him.

With lips pursed slightly, Mrs. Vickers gazed at her daughter a second or two before commenting. "Is it?"

"Now, Lesley," Mr. Vickers began.

"I know what you're going to say, Ted, so please don't. You're happy with anything the kids do. But why couldn't she try something different for a change?"

"I tried field hockey. That was different," Caroline replied.

"You know what I mean. Why couldn't you try out for the Debate Club or—cheerleading— something *really* different."

Caroline clutched Amber to her bosom in an oppressive headlock. The small dog whined in discomfort. "Sorry, girl," Caroline whispered, stroking her pet's head in appeasement. "Mom—we've gone over this before. I'm doing what I like best." Caroline sighed.

"I'm afraid I agree, Les. You and Caroline have been argue . . . excuse me," he said teasingly, "discussing this for quite a while. Her mind's made up so let's be happy for her. It's not every day a sophomore gets picked to play on the Varsity Squad." He walked over and silenced his wife with a quick kiss on the lips. "Let's not spoil the evening. Finish your sherry now and it's off to dinner," he smiled.

Looking at her father, Caroline smiled her gratitude. The small birthmark under his left eye highlighted the twinkle of conspiracy she saw there as he furtively winked at her.

"Well, I see I'm outnumbered, so I guess I'd better drop the subject," her mother said with a rueful smile. "By the way, Caroline, I think you have some mail."

Caroline placed Amber on the floor and crossed to the coffee table across from her mother and sorted through the remaining mail not yet opened. *I think?* Caroline was well aware her mother always knew who received mail and from where.

Sitting on the sofa opposite her mother, Caroline opened her letter and quickly read its contents.

"My first recruitment letter," she said, waving it gaily in the air. "They want me to consider the state university when college time rolls around."

"Well, isn't that something," Mr. Vickers said with obvious pride. It was Mrs. Vickers who asked to see the letter first and her expression as she read it was less than enthusiastic.

"I can't believe this, Ted. Caroline's only a sophomore. She's got two years before she goes to college," Mrs. Vickers said thrusting the letter at her husband to read. "Isn't it a little early for something like this?"

Mr. Vickers scanned the letter before he spoke. "Now, Lesley, it's just a typical recruitment letter. It may be a little soon but Caroline's a very good athlete and the local people have heard of her. They just want to get their bid in early, that's all. Competition is fierce between colleges and Caroline would be an asset for any women's program, since she can play more than one sport, and quite well I might add," he said smiling at his daughter. "Now let's go to dinner. Our reservation's in twenty minutes."

Mr. Vickers handed the letter back to Caroline and put on his coat, which had been lying across the back of the sofa.

"I still don't like it, Ted," Mrs. Vickers frowned. "And unless Caroline can get her geometry grades up I'm not so sure she should even be playing basketball at all."

Caroline was dumbfounded. She had heard of bad news traveling fast, but how could her mother know about that? Report cards weren't due for a while yet; besides, she saw it first and brought it home herself.

As if reading her mind, Mrs. Vickers answered her unspoken question. "Your geometry teacher sent us a note saying you were barely getting by and should consider a tutor."

Rising from her seat she approached her husband, anticipating his question too. "It only arrived this afternoon, Ted. You were dead tired earlier and I didn't want to discuss it tonight anyway and spoil our evening."

"Fine," Mr. Vickers said and helped his wife into her coat. "Then we won't discuss it tonight and spoil our evening and Caroline's.

We'll discuss it this weekend after everyone's had a chance to think about it."

Taking his wife's arm, Mr. Vickers picked up her pocketbook and opened the front door. "There's a casserole in the oven, kids," he yelled over his shoulder and then they were gone, leaving Caroline so stupefied she could barely wish them a nice evening.

Boy, Mr. Jeffers has really been working overtime, Caroline thought, collapsing in frustration on her chair.

"I couldn't help but overhear," Kurt said. Caroline looked up to see her brother enter the room and drop his lanky frame in front of the fireplace. "Mom's timing is lousy, but she is really thinking of you, kiddo."

That was the last straw. "I suppose *you* want me to be a cheerleader, too," she said sarcastically.

"What! Caroline Vickers a cheerleader? Heaven forbid!" he chuckled.

"It's not funny, Kurt," Caroline said. Then she added guardedly, "Do you think I should give up basketball, Kurt?"

"No. I don't. But I do think, if your grades are hurting you'd better do something about it and fast, before you get in over your head," Kurt said seriously.

"But Kurt, you know I'm no good in math," she replied in exasperation. "I've always been terrible in it and geometry is really hard for me. There are so many rules to remember I can't keep them straight."

"But if you fail geometry, what's the alternative?" Kurt persisted.

Passing a finger across her throat Caroline slumped across her chair in defeat. "I'm dead," she muttered. "The coach already told me she'll have no choice but to kick me off the team." She rose from her precarious perch and flung herself across the sofa. "Oh, Kurt," she said with a tremor in her voice. "Why does life have to be so darned difficult?"

"I don't know. But if it were easy, life sure would be dull."

Caroline looked at her brother more closely. "Do you really believe that?" she asked.

"No, but I asked dad the same question once, and that's what he told me," he laughed.

"Oh, you!" Caroline cried and she threw the pillow lying next to her, barely missing the crackling flames inside the fireplace. In seconds the pillow was a flying projectile whizzing back and forth across the room. Amber got caught up in the excitement and began following the pillow in its flight in a useless attempt to catch it. Her furious barking was deafening. Finally Kurt called a truce. Rising from the floor with Amber nipping at his pant leg, he walked over and pulled Caroline from her place of refuge behind the sofa. Then in a rare brotherly gesture, he draped an arm around her shoulders and kissed her cheek.

"Come on," he said and together they walked toward the kitchen. "Let's heat up that casserole and eat. And don't worry," he smiled down at her. "Things will get better. You'll see."

4

The early morning sun seeped through the blinds and curtains in Caroline's bedroom despite her efforts the night before to close them tightly. Originally, she had planned to sleep late. Wasn't that what weekends were for? Besides, after the hectic events of the last two weeks, she needed the rest. She felt as though she had been pulled in a hundred directions. Her mind was riding a roller coaster of incredible highs and depressing lows. One minute she was fine, the next she felt like crying her eyes out.

First, it had been her mother's nagging.

"Good intentions . . . for your own benefit . . . only thinking of you . . . etc." Then there had been Beth and Sheila's disappointing decision to branch out. Finally, there had been Mr. Jeffers's uncalled-for note to her parents. Notifying M.C. of low grades was one thing and in full accordance with school policy, but telling her parents was another. That was just something he had done on his own to "help her before things got out of hand." Well, quite frankly, he hasn't done me any favors, Caroline thought.

Flipping over onto her stomach, she balled her fists and pounded her pillows in frustration. Drat that man! Why did he have to be such a busybody, anyway? Who asked him to butt in? What good will geometry do me four or five years from now—a lifetime from now, she questioned.

Pulling the lavender blankets more tightly around her, she ducked under them, hoping she'd be able to block the sun's rays and at least be able to catch a little cat nap. But as hard as she tried she only succeeded in becoming more awake. She was trying too hard and annoying herself in the process.

Lying flat on her back with the blankets still over her head, she thought she'd give an old yoga exercise a try. She took several deep breaths to cleanse and slow her breathing. After a short amount of time, she began concentrating on relaxing her body. She concentrated on her toes, flexing them, willing them to relax. Then she focused on her calves and the tightness she felt there, trying to ease away the tension. Next she concentrated on her knees. She slowly continued the exercise working her way up her body, but in minutes she knew she was wasting her time. She was wearing herself out, not getting sleepy. She was using too much energy trying to block distracting thoughts from her mind, thoughts that were playing havoc with her emotions.

Her friends' decision not to play basketball was still upsetting, though she tried hard to accept it. Her feelings for Matt were becoming increasingly confused. Their last conversation had been stilted and disappointing for both of them. She hadn't spoken to him in the past couple of days—not because she didn't want to. Matt was keeping a low profile. However, the main source of aggravation was still her mother. Mrs. Vickers had voiced her objections quite plainly before and during tryouts. Caroline was sure she was still determined to scuttle her plans to play. Caroline was worried. It was bad enough that her mother wanted her to quit basketball. If her father joined forces with her, she was doomed. Although Mr. Vickers saw the benefits of athletics more clearly than his wife, he was also a stickler for good grades. Caroline somehow managed a B-minus average last year, much to her own surprise. If her grades slipped disastrously, he would probably insist she quit the team too. To top it all off, Caroline was having doubts. She still wanted to play basketball. She just wasn't sure she deserved to be on the Varsity Squad. M.C. was obviously counting on her to be a key player on the team. "A unifying force," the coach had said. But could she do it?

A sigh escaped Caroline's lips. The day wasn't even underway and already she felt tense. There was so much she had to do. And wasn't she supposed to meet Sheila and Beth today as well?

Wave after wave of confused thoughts rippled through her mind compounding the frustration and anxiety she felt. Frantically, her mind searched for a safe shore. Matt! As far as she was concerned he was the only good thing in her life right now, even though she hadn't spoken to him lately.

Yesterday, after her talk with Coach Cooper, Caroline and Valerie had celebrated their Varsity selection—at Friendly's, naturally. Caroline had hoped Matt would be there even though they hadn't made any arrangements to meet. Her expectations should not have been so high. It just would have been nice to have him share in her triumph. She felt as though she hadn't seen him in ages and sorely missed his smiling face.

During her silent reflection on the previous evening's events, Caroline suddenly remembered. She had planned to meet Beth and Sheila today at ten-thirty for an hour or two of horseback riding. Peeking out from under the blankets, she spied her clock radio flashing 9:05, Thank goodness! She had more than enough time to get ready.

Caroline had always enjoyed horseback riding and she was glad to be getting together with her friends. The invitation to go riding was definitely one of yesterday's unexpected highlights.

As Caroline and Valerie had been leaving Friendly's Beth and Sheila had been coming in. Circumstances were still awkward between the threesome. Just a week or two earlier the three of them would have been out on the town enjoying each other's company.

Nervously, Caroline awaited the worst, but nothing out of the ordinary occurred. To her surprise and pleasure their initial conversation went easily enough; then Beth and Sheila suggested horseback riding. They hadn't done this in weeks and Beth and Sheila even included Val, though they didn't know her from Eve. Unfortunately, Val had made other plans but their friendly gesture spurred Caroline to accept.

It was only after the good-byes were said and she and Val were headed homeward, that Caroline admitted the truth to herself. She had truly missed her two pals. They had been a part of her life for so long it was hard to break free, and in all honesty she didn't want to.

Curled in a tight little ball (your basic fetal position, according to her health instructor) Caroline couldn't help but think how ironic it would be, if just as she and her girlfriends got back together, her relationship with Matt fell apart. Just thinking about Matt caused goose-bumps to pop up all over her body. He was one in a million. But what could she do about him? He seemed so disappointed when she had to turn down his after-school invitations. She felt their relationship was coming un-glued at the seams, after everything had been so perfect between them. Things changed once basketball tryouts started, but she couldn't help it. They both had their own personal commitments to attend to besides the time they wanted to spend with each other.

Of the two of them, Matt's undertakings were more flexible but there was a reluctance on his part to change his plans when they conflicted with hers. Before they had always done things when he wanted to and that was fine with Caroline since it fit into her plans. Now things were different. She had tryouts to go to, just as she would have to go to daily team practices once they started. She also had homework to do. When else was she going to do it except after basketball? She couldn't hang out most of the evening. By the time she was through, most of the evening was shot anyhow. She had things to do and very little time to do them in. Matt would understand that, wouldn't he? All of a sudden her entire life was up in the air and it was driving her bonkers. But that was crazy. Just last week she had been on cloud nine. She had been excitingly anticipating basketball tryouts and still in a euphoric state over Matt.

Actually, things hadn't been that great between Caroline and Matt since their last date on Saturday. It was her first honest to goodness evening date with a guy she liked without the helping hand of one of her cronies setting things up. With eyes closed, Caroline could almost smell the dampness of the library air. She had spent most of the day cooped up in a second floor reading room at the local library working on her history paper. She was almost finished, which made her feel good.

It was a brilliant day after the heavy rain-

storms of the night before. Fluffy white clouds
dotted the aqua blue sky and paraded by
the reading room's partially opened window.
The crisp October breeze wafting through the
stacks reminded Caroline of what she was
missing. The days were shorter and cooler and
in no time it would be too cold to enjoy a
leisurely bike ride through the streets of Glendale. There would be no romping through the
fallen leaves lining Meetinghouse Lane with
Amber at her heels. The leaves would be
gone, scattered to the wind like a fading melo-
dy. The streets would be stark and barren
instead of warm and inviting as they were
now. Caroline didn't remember how many
times her father said, "Life isn't easy. Sometimes you have to bite the bullet." Well—
staying indoors to write a term paper on a
Saturday was biting the bullet all right. The
only thing that kept her going was her date
with Matt. It was going to be a beautiful
evening if it all worked out.

It had been easy to get Matt to agree to pick
her up at the library instead of at home. As
her paper was due in two weeks she had to
finish the bulk of it if she was going to have it
ready in time. She had decided to get to the
library early in the morning and work straight
through to three or so. By then, she would
definitely need a break, so she could go home,

grab a quick snack, change her clothes and still have enough time to return to the library for a couple more hours of work before their date. When Matt suggested she just remain at home and work, only Caroline's quick thinking saved the day. She told Matt there were just too many distractions at home. On a Saturday afternoon her house was like Grand Central Station. Her brother was sure to have friends gallivanting all over the place, his stereo cranked up full blast. The TV was always a temptation. She couldn't pass up those afternoon creature double features! And who could resist Amber? Once those luminous brown eyes looked into hers, she was like putty in her paws. Laughingly, Matt agreed her concentration would be at a minimum. He could always meet her folks once he dropped her off later that night.

Keeping Matt a secret was weird, she knew, but she wanted it that way. If her mother couldn't be supportive of her and her aspirations, then Caroline wouldn't share her life with her. The shame of it all was in keeping Matt from meeting her father. They'd get along splendidly together. They were the same type of person. Matt was active and outgoing and so was Mr. Vickers. He loved being around young people; that was one reason his real estate agency sponsored softball and football teams each year for the town's youngsters. Last year, he had even organized a Frisbee tournament for Glendale's 4th of July celebration and surprised everyone by doing a couple of fancy spins and catches himself. Eternally young, that was her father, and she couldn't wait for him to meet Matt. As for her mother, that was another story.

Flipping the covers off her face, Caroline stared at the ceiling. She realized she had denied her mother exactly what she wanted to see—her daughter dating and becoming popular among the crowd that counted. What better proof of this new-found popularity than Caroline's dating a well-known football star?

Caroline flung her arms across her eyes as if to fend off the guilt she felt. She hated to think of how she was deceiving her parents. She told them she had made a pact with Beth and Sheila. They were all going to spend the day working on their respective homework assignments and then as a reward, they were going to the movies together. Afterward they would treat themselves to a fattening ice cream sundae. It was "ladies' night out." Beth's parents would drive them.

Caroline's story was plausible. The Vickers were pleased and amused by their daughter's academic diligence. Before too long they were recounting tales of their youth in high school and college. They really got into the spirit of the evening, phony as it was, and Caroline could only sit and feel guilty. She wanted to tell them the truth, but couldn't face the consequences. Not then. Her parents were firm believers in grounding. It would be a long time before her weekends were her own again, if she spilled the beans. She only hoped her date with Matt was worth all of this deception. But even if it were, Caroline knew she had lost something that wouldn't be recaptured—a feeling of trust between her and her parents.

Stretching her lithe young body, Caroline basked in the memory of her date with Matt. Despite a tawdry beginning, her evening with him was even more wonderful than she could have ever dreamed. Everything had gone perfectly and their evening had been one she'd cherish forever.

Matt had arrived at the library promptly at seven and again Caroline had been struck by his dashing good looks. Dressed in brown tweed slacks, a cream cableknit turtleneck, and brown leather jacket, he looked older and more sophisticated than usual. His smile was warm and his touch gentle as he helped her into his '68 Camaro convertible. Second-hand and recently purchased, under Matt's tender loving care it looked practically brand-new and was his pride and joy.

A shiver of excitement passed through her

as they took the Old Bridge Road out of Glendale to Highway 295. They were headed toward a nearby university to see its film series on Redford and Newman. For the past week they had shown double features coupling each actor's more popular films. A friend of Matt's had gotten them tickets for that night. It was the last and undoubtedly the best night of the series and bound to be a sell-out.

The ride to the university was spent catching up on each other's day. Matt was very attentive. He wanted to know all about her paper and was pleased to hear she was almost finished. Sneaking a glance at his profile Caroline couldn't help but feel a warm glow all over. Would he always affect her like this? She didn't know. But at that moment she couldn't imagine it any other way.

By the end of the evening Caroline was in seventh heaven. The films had been super and the campus bistro had just the right atmosphere for a late meal and pleasant conversation. She had encouraged his talking and Matt had shared his future plans with her. He wasn't just a "dumb jock" as he told her, and really resented that generalization. He was an honor roll student and wanted to be a lawyer someday. His eager eyes glowed above the sputtering candle on their table. Would he ever achieve his goal? She longed to somehow know his future—be a part of it. But that was many years down the road and anything could happen in the meanwhile. It was a sad thought and she quickly dismissed it. The evening was made for laughter and good times. She planned to squeeze every last drop of both from it.

It was close to one-thirty by the time Matt parked in front of her home. The front light was on but the rest of the house slept in darkness. The evening had been beautiful. She had had more fun with Matt in a few hours than she had had all week. Only her present apprehension threatened to spoil the evening. Now that it was time to say goodnight, Caroline wasn't sure what she should say or do. She didn't want to appear foolish or immature. The words did not come easily but somehow she managed to mumble her thanks. With head bent she blushed at her own inadequacy. She could feel her cheeks become warmer and warmer. All of her conniving and she had blown it in just a few short minutes with her own shyness.

All was quiet inside the small vehicle. The only sound Caroline heard was her own rapidly beating heart. The pounding was so thunderous to her own ears that Caroline was positive Matt heard it too. Silently, she waited for him to say something. She raised her hand to unlock the door. Her unexpectedly abrupt movement caused the leather seating to shift. Cool fingers caressed and gently raised her chin. Caroline didn't have time to be nervous or afraid before Matt kissed her. The gentleness of the kiss was breathtaking. It wasn't a passionate entrapment that threatened to suffocate her but a tender touching. Too soon, however, the kiss ended and Matt slowly slid back to his side of the car.

"I had a great time," he said simply. "We've got to do this again . . . and soon."

As they strolled up the walk, Caroline thought how foolish she had been to keep Matt from meeting her parents. Here was someone intelligent, kind, as well as handsome. And he liked her! . . . Here was someone to be proud of, not hidden away—for any reason. Now she would happily introduce Matt to her parents, no matter what the consequences later. But as she unlocked the front door, she knew it wasn't to be. The interior of the house was as still as its outward appearance. Her parents had not waited up for her. Not even Amber came running down the stairs to share in her happiness. Caroline was crestfallen. Even a final embrace within Matt's arms could not still the haunting thought that an important moment had been lost.

* * *

Insistent scratching disrupted Caroline's thoughts later that night as she lay in bed. With the aid of a helping hand (probably Kurt's) the door opened. A panting butterball of fur barrelled across the floor and bounded onto her bed. Who said a dog's life was such a bad deal anyway? The way her life was going she'd trade places anytime.

5

It was close to eleven-fifteen by the time Caroline, Beth, and Sheila pedaled onto the grounds of Montgomery's stables. Dressed in an oversized, brilliant red wool turtleneck, faded blue jeans, and mud-encrusted boots (from her last outing), Caroline exalted in the short bike ride to the stables.

The sun was warm on her face and flickered brightly through the overhanging branches sheltering Glendale's residential streets. Within fifteen minutes the housing plots thinned out and the neatly paved asphalt roads gave way to a more rugged and graveled thorough-fare.

That was one of the things Caroline liked most about Glendale. For a suburban central New Jersey town, it had a lot to offer. Plush multi-store malls were readily available on its outskirts. Quick access to New York City, which was only two hours away, was possible. And a country atmosphere could be easily had without driving a long distance to get there.

Spacious threshed fields trimmed the road-way as the girls rode toward their destination. The sallow color of the fields rimmed by the autumnal relief of close knit trees reminded Caroline that Halloween was just around the corner, and the Sadie Hawkins Dance soon after. For a while Caroline had allowed her-self to dream that she and Matt would attend together. Now that all seemed wishful think-ing.

As she rode along with her friends Caroline was struck by the naturalness of the camara-derie she felt. It was as if by unspoken agree-ment, the threesome had decided to forget the past couple of weeks and start anew. Bol-stered by the beauty of the morning and the happiness she felt by being with her two friends, Caroline silently vowed not to let anything come between them ever again, if they could again be the close friends they once were.

It had taken awhile, but Caroline was beginning to realize that Beth and Sheila were not the traitors, as she had subconsciously labeled them. They were still her friends. They were just changing. And luckily that change didn't mean growing totally apart and not wanting to be with each other.

Exhilarated by their bike ride, the three girls were ready for a speedy gallop across the fields and wooded acreage surrounding the stables. They rode up the dirt drive and propped their bicycles against the side of the farmhouse before going in search of Mr. Montgomery.

Day in and day out you could rely on Mr. Montgomery to be there. He rarely took vacations and never seemed to tire of his job. During the week he usually worked alone since only those persons who boarded a horse were about. On the weekends, the traffic was heavier and extra help was needed. The weekend was the time when a lot of "urban cowboys" and "landed gentry" came out to practice their equestrian skills.

Though small in comparison to its neighbors, Montgomery's did a thriving business, offering Western and English riding for the would-be horseman. Lessons could be purchased, but if Mr. Montgomery wasn't busy, he gladly offered some friendly, free advice to the novice.

The stable grounds had a lot of character and the varying shades of fall's foliage surrounding the stables was breathtaking. The buildings themselves weren't fancy and new or covered with aluminum siding. Montgomery's was more rustic. It was comfortable and weathered, like a cherished pair of well-worn jeans. Montgomery's was what a stable *should* look like, Caroline thought, and the girls always felt welcomed whenever they came.

As the trio walked in search of assistance, they saw a small group of female riders being led around the barn. With just a back view to observe, and that more of horseflesh than anything else, neither Caroline nor her friends could identify the riders.

In a leisurely fashion, the threesome crossed the dusty distance to the back of the barn. The crisp morning air was refreshing and the mid-morning sun warmed their faces, as they reminisced of their last trip to the stables.

Approaching the corner of the barn they noticed the bevy of riders they had just glimpsed moments before coming toward them. Upon closer inspection, Caroline recognized them. They were juniors at Glendale and members of the group that practically "ran" the junior class. You'd never catch *them* sweating on a basketball court or standing in the back of a high school chorus line. They were more politically and socially motivated.

The blonde in the center was Elaine Kennedy, vice president of the Student Council, the petite redhead to the left was Lisa Bentley—treasurer of the school's Social Committee and chairwoman of the committee handling this year's Sadie Hawkins Dance. And of course Caroline recognized the twins, tall, lanky, curly-haired brunettes, Sharon and Karen Scott. They were ex-cheerleaders who dated, respectively, the captain of the basketball team and the captain of the football team.

This foursome, along with a few others, dictated what and who was acceptable at Glendale. They were the trendsetters and getting onto "their team" wasn't easy. Every class had their "in crowd" and some people spent their entire high school career trying to make the grade. Caroline and her friends were different. They did *what* they wanted, *when* they wanted to because it was fun, not because it was socially acceptable or the "in" thing to do. Socially, as underclassmen they weren't in the same league as the foursome coming toward them. They weren't friends with the foursome, but they weren't rivals either. They knew each other and the social strata they belonged to—a vaguely defined area that separates an "acquaintance" from a total stranger. Usually, an offhanded "hi" was the extent of the social interaction between the two groups' members. Today, however, was different and the behavior of the upperclassmen was odd to say the very least.

Stranger still were the nudging and whispering that seemed to be centered around Lisa. They were still far enough away that none of the trio could hear what was being said. But it was obvious from the looks and gestures that at least *one* of the trio was the subject of conversation.

No one said a word as the two groups slowly reached each other. However, it was Beth who seized the moment and spoke up just as the elder girls passed.

"It's a shame some parents don't teach their children that it's rude to gawk at people," she said loudly.

A barely audible gasp was heard from behind them as each group continued on its way.

"I wonder what that was all about," Caroline said. "Maybe the twins were pointing you out, Sheila. After all, you may be replacing one of them on the cheerleading squad."

"Hmmmm—could be," her friend replied thoughtfully.

"It really doesn't matter *why*," Beth emphasized. "They were *rude*. *Period* . . . but at least *one* of them had the decency to be embarrassed," she giggled, causing Beth and Sheila to laugh too.

Good old Beth, Caroline thought fondly. She can find the humor in any situation. Affectionately she patted her friend on the back. Out of sheer happiness, she gave Beth a brief hug. Naturally, she couldn't neglect Sheila who stood by the sideline, and before long, they were all hugging each other and talking a mile a minute. Each one wanted to apologize; eyes misted as one after the other apologized for some real or imaginary offense.

The absurdity of the past few weeks had been dispelled by a single outside threat. Now all was forgiven—if not totally forgotten. The "three mousketeers" were together once more.

Caroline was too busy rejoicing in her rekindled friendships to notice Mr. Montgomery reclining on a stack of bales and calmly chewing a piece of hay.

"Haven't seen you young ladies here in a long time," Mr. Montgomery remarked. "Hope you're ready for a little exercise?" He smiled.

"You bet," they chorused.

"In that case, I'll give you a couple of real frisky mounts. You still remember how to ride, don't you?" he said jokingly.

Feigning indignation, each girl began talking at once in reply until Mr. Montgomery covered his ears and turned away in protest.

"Matt," he shouted. "Bring those two mares and Rocky over here before these young fillies talk my ears off."

Caroline felt everything was moving in slow motion. Calm down and don't be stupid, she told herself. There's more than one Matt on this earth. She took a couple of deep breaths in order to steady herself.

It was just when she had convinced herself and was about to join her friends that she saw him.

Varying degrees of dirt and straw covered his person, yet it gave him an earthiness she found very appealing. As he led the three horses to where Beth and Sheila stood chatting amicably with his boss, their eyes met momentarily. Caroline was not surprised to see a hint of reserve in his manner.

Her girlfriends were just mounting their horses. Caroline looked their way with mixed emotions. She wanted to be with them and didn't want to spoil their morning together. Yet, here was an opportunity to talk to Matt and she couldn't pass that up either. Frozen by indecision, she just stood there.

But Caroline need not have worried. Beth and Sheila had recognized Matt even before he walked up to them. They had seen Caroline and him together often enough the week before. They had heard the latest talk about the "new twosome" as well. What at first glance seemed to be a "hot romance" had cooled this last week and they were sure this was bothering their friend.

With that intuitive sense that close friendships bring, they understood the look of hesitation and confusion in Caroline's eyes.

"Hey, slowpoke," Sheila yelled, as Mr. Montgomery finished adjusting her stirrups. "Beth and I are going to warm up a bit and try a few low jumps."

Taking the cue, Beth added cheerfully, "We'll be in the front corral. Okay?"

"That's fine with me," Caroline said gratefully. Beth and Sheila, accompanied by Mr. Montgomery, headed for the corral.

"If you need any help with adjusting her stirrups," Mr. Montgomery shouted over his shoulder, "just give a whistle."

"No problem," Matt answered jovially.

Caroline and Matt silently watched the older man and young girls move away, leaving them alone.

At first, Matt didn't acknowledge her presence, but continued caressing the neck of a beautiful chestnut mare standing beside him.

How Caroline longed to change places with her and be on the receiving end of Matt's gentle caress! After a few seconds of more silence, she permitted her gaze to wander toward him. Fathomless blue eyes held her own. She felt faint and would have slithered to the ground if she hadn't been holding the mare's bridle. Swallowing quickly, she found her voice and returned his steady regard.

"Hi," she said to Matt in a small voice.

"Hi," he replied solemnly.

"She's a beauty," Caroline continued. "What's her name?"

"Chiclet."

"Oh, that's cute," she said. Then in the most natural tone she could muster, she said, "I didn't know you worked here. Have you been here long?"

"No, I just started this morning," he answered flatly and Caroline was struck by the lack of warmth and friendliness in his tone.

He's not making this easy, she thought. But still she persisted.

"Well, do you like it?" she asked lamely, then immediately thought, *how dumb*. That was a really stupid question. What can he say? He just started today. If Caroline could have vanished at that moment she would have gladly done so. Her ears were burning and she felt her face flushing. She wished the ground would swallow her up, so she wouldn't have to face the mocking look she was sure Matt was giving her.

"So far I like it fine," Matt replied casually.

The situation would have been funny if it

hadn't been so important to Caroline. Just a week earlier she and Matt couldn't say enough to each other. Now their conversation was clichéd and unbearably strained. That hurt Caroline. She didn't want to play games. Matt meant too much to her to do that. All she wanted was to know where they stood and there was only one way to find out. Caroline's pulse pounded frantically but she took the plunge and said what was utmost on her mind.

"I haven't seen much of you lately," she murmured. It was more a statement than a question but the meaning was apparent.

His look was incredulous. "Caroline," he began slowly. "I don't want to argue with you. But if you haven't seen a lot of me lately that's *your* fault, *not mine.*"

"Mine," Caroline gasped. "But I was dying to see you—"

"Well, you could have fooled me," he replied testily. "Every time I tried to see you last week you had basketball tryouts or you were too tired or something came up. If you don't want to be bothered with me just say so and let's make a clean break."

Caroline nervously shifted her weight from one leg to the other. She had never realized just how badly he had taken her refusal of his invitations.

"Oh Matt, I *do* want to be bothered. I'm not

avoiding you," she said. "I want to be with you as much as you want to be with me. Maybe more so," she said and her eyes lowered as a wave of shyness swept over her. She had never said anything like that to a boy before in her life; it was a little frightening. But she knew she must go on.

"It's just that there are so many things to be done. Some I *want* to do and others I *have* to do and sometimes there isn't enough time to do it all. *You* of *all people* should understand that," she said with a slight smile.

"What do you mean by that?"

"Well—we both have homework we have to do," Caroline said.

"Sure, we do," he interjected quickly. "But I'm still willing to make the time to see you."

"I know and I really appreciate that. I realize how important your studies are to you," and as she spoke she remembered how determinedly he spoke of becoming a lawyer one day. "And if *I* just had homework to do, it would be easier for me to rearrange my study schedule and make time *for you*. But that's not the case. I had basketball tryouts all last week and I couldn't miss them. I just found out yesterday that I made the Varsity basketball team and that means more practices and competition. You play football. You know what it's like during the season."

Matt was silent as he ran a hand through his hair disrupting the curls.

"I do want to see you," Caroline continued, "but my evenings are still going to be pretty tied up and that won't change for a long while—"

"But what about after basketball practice, Caroline?" Matt asked. "Maybe I'm being selfish, but I really don't think so. This is supposed to be a two-person relationship. I'm not asking for *all* your time. Just some of it. *You* have to make an effort too. Where there's a will there's a way. I guess it depends on how badly you really want to be with me."

Now it was Caroline's turn to be silent as she reflected on Matt's words. Could he possibly be right? She looked searchingly into his eyes, and stepped a little closer to him. Her tentative smile was answered by his own. "Matt," she whispered and her voice was unusually deep to her ears. "Can we start all over?"

The warming smile Matt gave her as he dropped the reins and clasped her hands was all the answer she needed. He was so close, she could see the little pulse beat on the side of his neck. Her vision blurred as he bent down and kissed her lightly on the lips.

It was Chiclet, her patience exhausted, who interrupted their happy reunion. One nudge from her sturdy head nearly sent them sprawling as she loudly whinnied her annoyance.

"Okay, girl, okay. You can have her for a little while." He grasped the reins to steady the mare and helped Caroline mount.

"But you bring her back in one piece you, you hear?" he said to the prancing horse. Both Matt and Caroline laughed when Chiclet nodded her head in seeming agreement.

The mounts provided Caroline and her friends were as frisky as Mr. Montgomery had promised. For over an hour the threesome cavorted across the stable grounds. They laughed as the wind whistled passed them while they galloped down wooded paths and tried to talk at the same time. Eventually, they came upon a quiet slope bordering the narrow creek that marked the boundary of Mr. Montgomery's property. They paused to admire the view and give their horses a breather.

Beth and Sheila had wanted to know every detail of Caroline's romance and now she was only too happy to comply. For a long time she had wanted to talk to someone her own age about Matt. Sheila and Beth had been her sounding boards in the past but over the last couple of weeks the situation had changed.

Now Caroline made up for lost time. She was too ashamed to tell them of how she used them as alibis to deceive her parents. But about everything else she was truthful. It all came tumbling out; it was as if she had mentally tape-recorded every conversation she had ever had with Matt.

Beth and Sheila giggled nervously as Caroline recalled how Matt had shyly asked her out. They blushed knowingly as she tried to explain the strange new feelings Matt aroused in her. They empathized with her difficulty in juggling boyfriend, homework, and basketball.

"A guy's ego can be *so* fragile," Beth said.

"Sometimes a relationship can be so complicated," Sheila interjected somberly. "You don't want to be selfish but sometimes you just want things done your way."

"Nobody wants to feel obligated to see someone but sometimes you just have to compromise in a relationship, especially if you *really and truly* like the guy," Beth concluded, and she looked at Caroline questioningly.

Caroline's eyes rested on the rippling water trickling past them. Then she gave Beth a shy smile. "Well, I *really and truly* do like Matt," she said in a low voice.

"Then it's good you and he talked things over and straightened things out. No relationship is perfect. But if you make the effort it can be well worth it," Beth replied with a wink.

"As long as you're happy," Sheila said. "You *are* happy, aren't you, Caroline?" she queried tentatively.

"More than I've ever been in my life!" was Caroline's enthusiastic response.

After their ride, the girls settled themselves comfortably at the Vickerses' kitchen table and gorged themselves on ham and cheese sandwiches. Mrs. Vickers had insisted that Beth and Sheila make themselves at home while she made all of them a late lunch.

Caroline could barely contain her astonishment at her mother's offer. She had wanted her to make new friends. She had almost come right out and said, "Drop Beth and Sheila. Your friends are holding you back," yet here she was happily waiting on them.

To her surprise, Mrs. Vickers even carried over a cup of coffee, pulled out a chair, and joined them. But this did not inhibit their conversation. Mrs. Vickers had 'a youthful outlook,' Caroline's girlfriends had always said, and they enjoyed talking to her, but this time Caroline felt uneasy.

Mrs. Vickers listened attentively as Beth told of her Glee Club audition and subsequent acceptance into the club. Her eyebrows raised slightly as Beth expressed excitement over meeting new friends. Caroline refused to meet her mother's gaze and busily poured herself another glass of milk.

Predictably, the conversation shifted to Sheila when Beth mentioned the upcoming cheerleading tryouts. Caroline felt her mother was showing a more than casual interest.

"Well, how do you like cheerleading so far?" Mrs. Vickers asked Sheila.

"Oh, it's great, Mrs. Vickers," Sheila answered. "But it's still just practice. Tryouts aren't until Wednesday and I have to admit I'm getting more and more nervous as the day gets closer. Some of those routines are really tough! And I still haven't perfected my split."

"Don't worry," Mrs. Vickers said. "You're an attractive girl. You're bound to be picked for the squad."

"Thanks for the vote of confidence, Mrs. Vickers." Sheila laughed. "But school spirit and enthusiasm are equally important. Looks won't do it all. I just hope I last until this is all over," she said with a sigh.

"I know you will," Mrs. Vickers assured her. "I still think looks and personality are important. Did you know Caroline's sister—Bobbi— was a cheerleader for Glendale?" she added.

With mouths full of sandwich Caroline's friends nodded in affirmation. "I'm sure her looks and personality helped *her* to be chosen, and she isn't any more attractive than you—*or Caroline* for that matter."

Caroline looked across suspiciously at her mother.

"In any event," Mrs. Vickers continued, "I don't think you have anything to worry about."

For a brief moment, all talk ceased as Mrs. Vickers and the girls consumed the lunch she had prepared.

"It's a shame," Mrs. Vickers broke the silence and all eyes again turned toward her. "It would be so nice if all of you tried out for the cheerleading squad. After all you've been friends for as long as I can remember."

"You know, it *would* be great if we all tried out. There *are* four spots open on the squad and we could all be doing something together," Sheila cried.

"Maybe, it *would* have been nice if we had thought of it earlier," Beth said pensively.

"It's too late now," Caroline interjected sharply. "There isn't enough time to learn the routines."

"Oh, surely you've seen them done enough," Mrs. Vickers said hopefully. "And if Sheila gave you a little help, you could be ready for Wednesday's tryouts. You're attractive enough and it would be fun!"

"I'm sorry, mom, but there just isn't enough

time to learn the routines," Caroline spoke softly. "It was a nice thought anyway."

Caroline wasn't sure why she had added that. It implied she would have tried out for cheerleading if there had been time. She knew in her heart of hearts she never would have attempted such a thing.

"Yeah, it was a nice thought," agreed Beth between mouthfuls. "But to be honest, Mrs. Vickers, I really don't think I would have done it. Cheerleading's just not my style. You know what I mean? I'd feel like a klutz out there in front of all those people."

Caroline could have kissed her friend for her comments. If only she had stopped there!

"Don't worry, Mrs. Vickers," she continued, "Caroline may not go out for cheerleading but we have other things that occupy our time— especially Caroline," and she flashed her a lopsided grin.

"Really," said Mrs. Vickers. She leaned on the edge of her seat. "This *is* something new. What is it?"

The elfin grin which seconds earlier stretched happily across Beth's face rapidly disintegrated under Caroline's intense, warning stare.

"Well, don't keep me in suspense," Mrs. Vickers said. "What's occupying your time that's so wonderful these days?"

"Why basketball of course, mom. Remember?" Caroline said quickly. "I made the Varsity Squad."

The gleam of excitement that moments before shone brightly in Mrs. Vickers's eyes dimmed and a comic look of despair appeared in its place. "Caroline, as hard as I might try there's no way I could *possibly* forget that," Mrs. Vickers replied sarcastically.

Caroline had succeeded in turning the conversation away from Matt but she could not help feeling that there was very little she could discuss anymore with her mother.

6

During the next several days, Mother Nature kicked up her skirts and buffeted central New Jersey with high winds and thunderstorms. Telephone lines fell, windows blew out, and there were many minor flash floods.

While surrounding towns suffered damages, Glendale escaped virtually untouched. A few loose tiles blew off roofs and one or two trees toppled, but mostly the chaotic force of wind and rain only hastened the descent of dying leaves.

The past weekend had been a revelation for

Caroline. She realized the importance of her friendship with Beth and Sheila. She appreciated her girlfriends all the more for the support they had given her in spite of her recent coldness to them.

On Sunday afternoon, she finally had the opportunity to explain the secrecy surrounding her relationship with Matt to her friends. Picking up the upper hall phone, Caroline slumped to her bedroom floor, shut the door, and filled in all the gaps while Beth and Sheila shared the latter's bedroom extension.

At first her friends listened silently. Only their breathing was audible as Caroline rambled, grateful for the opportunity to share her troubled thoughts. She knew she could rely on her friends to tell her the truth without too much sugarcoating.

True to their record, Beth and Sheila were tactful but they agreed; Caroline was treading in dangerous waters by deceiving her parents and hiding her relationship with Matt. Caroline had always been close to both her parents, they reminded her. It was a closeness built upon mutual love and trust. Did she realize how hurt Mr. and Mrs. Vickers would be if they ever found out about Caroline's "sneaking around," as Beth so grossly put it?

Instinctively, they knew Caroline had been trying to hurt her mother just as she had been hurt. Her silence about Matt had been her only of "getting back" at her mother. If Mrs. Vickers couldn't accept the things that made Caroline happy and be proud of her accomplishments, then they could understand why Caroline didn't tell her mother about Matt. Caroline was conducting her own silent rebellion but it wasn't making her happy, her friends told her. It was obvious to them Caroline was miserable over the whole thing. So why continue?

"You know you're not really hurting your mother anyway," Beth said with caution. "She doesn't know about Matt and you can't hurt someone if they don't know whatever it is you're keeping from them."

"And anyway," Sheila jumped in, "does it matter *now*? You're on the Varsity Squad. You have Matt. And your mom can no longer pressure you to be a cheerleader. I mean she could but it's too late for you to try out this year and she knows it. So . . . there's no reason to keep Matt a secret, is there?"

Caroline pondered her friend's words. Was there a reason for continuing the charade? She had lied in the first place only to retaliate for the "bad time" she felt her mother was giving her. But in a manner of speaking, she *had won*, hadn't she? She hadn't lost a thing, except possibly her self-respect. Thinking of this, Caroline flushed with embarrassment. The bottom line was that Caroline *did* have basketball *and Matt*. What more could she ask for?

A small nervous giggle slipped passed Caroline's lips.

"Are you all right?" Beth asked warily over the phone.

"Never better," Caroline happily replied. "And you're right. I do have everything I wanted from the very beginning. There is no reason for me to keep Matt a secret."

By late that evening, however, Caroline's exuberance was threatened by the inevitable. Mr. and Mrs. Vickers were finally ready to discuss the note Mr. Jeffers had sent them. The dining room was the customary setting for all important family discussions and this was definitely *one of those*.

Caroline could barely hide her apprehension as she entered the dining room with loyal Amber trotting at her heels. Sensing her mistress's uneasiness, Amber attached herself to Caroline and would have remained at her side but her constant movement and tail wagging promised to be a distraction that could not be tolerated.

"I want to be sure *everybody's* attention is on the subject at hand and not this little nuisance," Mr. Vickers chided jokingly. In one deft motion he picked up Amber, deposited her in the kitchen, and shut the door much to her whimpering displeasure. Then he joined his wife on one side of the table and Caroline sat on the other.

Strategically speaking the seating arrangement was a bit overpowering, but as Mr. Vickers cleared his throat Caroline noted that neither he nor her mother seemed angry, which put her at ease a little.

"Look, Carrie," her father began. "You know math isn't easy for you and we know it isn't easy for you, but we don't want you using that as an excuse. Can you honestly say you've been keeping up with your geometry studies?"

"No, dad. I haven't kept up with geometry. I *am* a little behind," she said softly. "But," she was quick to add, "that's only because I've been spending a lot of time on my history paper. It's due a week from tomorrow but I wanted to finish it early before the basketball season got into full swing. I'm just about through now. All I have to do is type it—" Her excuse sounded feeble even to herself.

"Well *that's* good," her mother said with a smile. "You're on top of one subject. But what about the rest?" she prodded. "The fact remains you're barely holding your head above water in geometry."

"You really need to concentrate your efforts on that for a while, honey," Mr. Vickers added kindly.

"It's all in the way you organize your daily schedule," Mrs. Vickers said. "If you didn't have basketball practice it would be easier to find more study time. However, your father . . . and I," she added with a faint smile, "have decided to let you continue with your plans to play on the basketball team—at least for a while."

Thank goodness, Caroline sighed inwardly. Saved. But what does *for a while mean*? She didn't have long to wait before she found out the answer.

"On the condition that," Mr. Vickers continued firmly, "we see some improvement in your geometry grades. According to Mr. Jeffers you're having a quiz on Friday and we want you to be ready. You've got five days—including today—to get it together. So you'd better start hitting the books right away. After your quiz, we'll see how things shape up. Okay?"

It was a rhetorical question. Caroline had no choice. It could have been worse. She could have been saying a fond farewell to basketball by now; instead she had a chance to continue playing the game she loved.

Though the meeting with her parents was over, Caroline remained seated and contemplated her course of action. Not even Amber, freed from the confines of the kitchen, could distract her. Caroline felt as though she had been given a reprieve and she was determined to make the most of it. She wanted it all—basketball, Matt, *and* good grades.

She had to admit she'd been sloughing off lately. But sports were so much more fun than studying! Other students, no brighter than herself, managed to balance schoolwork, dates, and extracurricular activities and she didn't see any reason why she couldn't do the same. Improving her geometry grades would also please her parents and make up for some of the lies she had told them. They wouldn't know it, of course, but she would; it would help her to feel better about herself.

Tomorrow I'm starting out fresh, she told herself enthusiastically. *It'll be a new Caroline Vickers you'll see in your class, Mr. Jeffers.* She leapt from the table and bounded up the stairs to begin her studies.

If Matt was surprised by Caroline's invitation to meet her parents when he picked her up after her Monday practice it was an equal surprise to Mr. and Mrs. Vickers. Since Caroline had never mentioned Matt, the sight of the tall good-looking athlete gracing their living room entry was a bit of a shock, but "a pleasant surprise nevertheless," Mrs. Vickers said with feeling not lost on Caroline. Mr. Vickers was more low-keyed with his welcome but warmed to Matt quickly. By the time dinner was over, for Mrs. Vickers had insisted he stay for it, they were laughing and joking with ease, just as Caroline had hoped they would.

Caroline's relationship with Matt was on good footing these days and she happily discovered the initial companionability she felt with Matt was still intact. Their evening meetings recaptured the fun of their earlier dates and it was during one of their late evening outings that Caroline discovered something else too. She was in love with Matt. The feeling had been haunting her for some time, though she had been hard pressed to pin a label to it. Now she understood why he was never far from her thoughts and why she was so motivated to please him. Matt wasn't just a guy she liked. He was the guy for her.

Caroline's acceptance of her love for Matt brought added excitement into her life. Their clandestine relationship was out in the open and it was a heady experience for her. She wanted their relationship to be perfect. But she didn't want to sacrifice her grades or basketball. Of her three "problems," basketball was the least complicated.

Once Caroline was out on the basketball court and starting her warm-up exercises, she quickly became too involved to think about anything else. With each drill, jumpshot, and scrimmage, Caroline could feel herself improving. It was a natural high and she loved it. In a way basketball was her refuge. When she was on the court nothing else mattered and all problems were forgotten—at least momentarily. It was off the court that Caroline had difficulties and they began with geometry.

Caroline didn't stop to talk to her fellow classmates when she entered the geometry class on Monday, but instead moved swiftly to her seat. She leaned down to stow away the books she wouldn't need under her seat. When she straightened, she smoothed her hair away from her brow and saw Mr. Jeffers walk into the room.

Short, slender, and with graying hair at the temples, he looked the epitome of a high school teacher in his houndstooth jacket with patched elbows and glasses stuffed in the breast pocket. He was a popular teacher despite his old-fashioned ideas and Caroline watched silently as he conversed with his students.

At the sound of the warning bell, Mr. Jeffers smilingly urged the students to their seats. He sat at his desk and placed his books in front of him. Caroline watched his eyes search the throng of students until they settled on her. Nervously Caroline looked away just as he looked as if he were going to speak to her.

Then a late arriving student barged in, attracting his attention, and the moment was gone. Caroline was glad for the interruption and quickly buried herself in her books. She didn't want to talk to anyone right then, especially Mr. Jeffers. She still resented the note to her parents. She planned on keeping her distance until after the quiz. Caroline was determined Mr. Jeffers would be so stunned by her great test score that he'd have to apologize for writing her parents. But right now, she just wanted to be left alone.

By Wednesday, in spite of the goals she'd set for herself, Caroline's inner resolve was shaken. She didn't know what she had expected to happen in so short a time but her performance had been disappointing. For the first two days of the week, she had remained inconspicuous behind the broad shoulders of the boy in front of her. But at the end of Wednesday's class her luck ran out and Mr. Jeffers called on her. She felt he had deliberately singled her out for public ridicule. Embarrassed and annoyed, she couldn't even bluff her way through the answer. She hadn't studied that section of the book the night before; she barely understood his in-class explanation of a similar problem; so she simply stared at her books and simmered in silence. Fortunately, another student volunteered the answer, then the bell marking the period's end rang and Caroline rushed to escape. However, when she reached the top of her aisle Mr. Jeffers had called to her.

"Can I see you for a moment, Ms. Vickers?" he asked pleasantly.

In a brief instant of defiance, Caroline considered pretending she hadn't heard him but too many students were blocking the doorway, making a hasty exit impossible. He casually moved to the front of his desk and sat on its edge with his hands resting peacefully on his knees. "This won't take long," he said. "And if I keep you after the next bell I'll write you a note. This morning I received a letter from your parents."

That's news to me, Caroline thought, but she remained silent.

"Your parents understand my concern for your grades and they say you've been studying hard. I would really like to see you do well on this quiz, Caroline, but I still get the feeling you're having problems. *Do* you need any help?"

"No thank you, Mr. Jeffers. I don't. I'm okay, really."

"Are you sure?" he persisted. "Don't be afraid or embarrassed to ask for help. If you need a tutor, I can get you one, although I wish you'd come to me sooner."

I wish you'd come to me sooner. Was Mr.

Jeffers offering help or chastizing her for waiting so long? Caroline wondered. "I'm fine, Mr. Jeffers. Thanks for your offer but I don't need a tutor," she said. "And I really have to go now or I'll be late for my next class."

"Well, all right then," he said as he hopped from the desk, removed his glasses and placed them in his pocket. "You should know if you need help or not. But remember, Caroline," he said as they walked into the hallway, "if you do need help there's no crime in asking for it."

By the fifth period Caroline was more than ready for lunch and sat apart from the more rowdy students while she waited for Beth and Sheila to arrive. She was too irritated to eat. She was irritated at Mr. Jeffers, her parents, but most of all at herself. Mr. Jeffers had offered her help and she had stubbornly refused, all because she hadn't liked the way he had handled things. He could have at least told me he was writing my folks. Not that it would have changed anything. But at least I would have known it was coming, she fumed angrily.

She resented his attitude. He had made her feel stupid to have waited so long without asking for help. But what was even more irritating was that she knew he had been right. She had wanted to do it all by herself and make everyone feel bad for "picking on her." But instead she cooked her own goose. *How could I have been so stupid,* she scolded herself. She propped her chin in her hands and stared into space. It was this dejected picture that greeted Beth and Sheila.

"Who rained on your parade?" Sheila asked in a concerned voice.

"Yeah," Beth added. "You're looking mighty low."

Suppressing the quivering in her lower lip, Caroline sadly looked at her friends.

"I just did something really stupid," she said tearfully. "Mr. Jeffers offered to get me help in geometry and like an idiot I turned him down."

Pushing their trays aside, Caroline's friends silently looked at one another until finally Beth spoke.

"Just how badly are you doing?" she asked solemnly. Caroline quickly explained her painstaking process of reviewing her homework assignments. She was afraid she wouldn't have enough time to learn it all. There were still things she didn't understand, and she only had two more evenings to mull through the work.

"Well, let's not throw in the towel so soon," Beth said. "It's not too late."

"But I can't go back now and tell Mr. Jeffers

I need help when I just got finished telling him I didn't need any," Caroline cried.

"Well, maybe you don't have to," Beth suggested. "My geometry class just finished covering some of the same material and I know it pretty well. We can get together after your practices the next couple of days and go over those areas where you're having problems."

"Oh could we?" Caroline appealed to her friend.

"Sure, easy. Don't sweat it," Beth said with certainty. "You'll be getting out of basketball practice early today since they'll be using the gym for the cheerleader tryouts at six. We can meet there and then head to my place . . . all right?"

Oh heavens, Caroline thought, forgetting her own problem for a moment. I forgot all about the cheerleading tryouts. Today's Sheila's big day.

Clutching her friend's hand Caroline gave her a shaky smile. "Sheila, I'm sorry. I completely forgot. Go out there tonight and break a leg," she laughed.

"With my luck I probably will, I'm so nervous," Sheila croaked.

"Don't worry. You'll be great. You'll see," Caroline replied.

"We'll both be fine," Sheila said lightly. "While I'm knocking them dead at the tryouts, you'll have some extra time tonight to study for that quiz you'll *pass on Friday,*" she emphasized.

"Oh, no," Caroline moaned. "My mind must be out to lunch. I have to meet Matt after practice tonight."

"You don't *have to* see him tonight," Beth emphasized. "Besides this is more important. If your grade doesn't improve, or, heaven forbid, if you fail the quiz it's bye, bye, basketball. Matt will understand that. *You have to study,* Slim. *You need to study.*"

There was nothing Caroline could say. She had to devote more time to her geometry or she wouldn't be ready for the quiz. It was time to do some serious cramming and unfortunately that would leave no time for Matt. She didn't want to break her commitment to see Matt after they had already planned to get together. Not to mention the fact she didn't want him to know she was in possible academic trouble. Matt was so smart. He probably breezed through geometry, she thought. And here I am struggling through it. He could have any girl he wants. He wouldn't want to go out with a dummy.

Scowling darkly Beth snapped Caroline from her private reverie. "Just tell him you have to study tonight. You have a test Friday and you have to hit the books. What's the big deal?"

"You're right," Caroline said. "This *is* important. I have to study and that's that," she said with conviction. "Matt will just have to understand."

After an energetic but brief practice Caroline stopped to briefly wish Sheila good luck, then showered, dressed, and raced from the locker room.

Stepping into the crowded hallway filled with the noisy activity of students awaiting the selection of the new cheerleaders Caroline searched in vain for a glimpse of Matt. It was her first opportunity to inform Matt of her change in plans and she was a little nervous, but she was also more positive about her decision. She could postpone seeing Matt because she needed this time for herself—for her studies. But she couldn't cut basketball if she wanted to play, especially now. Coach Cooper had managed to set up a scrimmage with the girls from Holy Cross High School for Friday after school. They were one of the best teams in the area and even though it was a scrimmage the team was psyched and they wanted to win.

This was a chance for each girl to show her stuff against some top-rank competition. A good performance would insure a starting position on the Varsity Squad and Caroline was just as excited and determined to do well as her teammates.

First things first though, Caroline murmured to herself. I have to pass that quiz first.

Spying Beth glued to the glass in a nearby
gym door, Caroline walked over and peered
in.

"How's Sheila doing?" she said with concern.

"Great!" was Beth's ear-shattering response. "She just got through her split with
no problem. She's going to make it! I just
know she is!" she squealed.

"Who's going to make it?" a deep voice
asked from nearby.

Turning suddenly Caroline found herself
facing Matt. Matt was an impressive figure in
any setting but he looked especially handsome
today in gray flannel slacks and a deep blue
cotton shirt that matched his eyes exactly. A
short distance behind him a group of his
friends stood waiting. Caroline recognized a
couple of Matt's football buddies. She had met
them once or twice before. But to her chagrin
she also noticed Lisa Bentley and the twins.

"Well, who's going to make it?" Matt asked
again with a grin. "*My* money's on the redhead on the right," he said with a smirk.

"Well, *our* money's on Sheila Richardson,"
Beth interjected confidently. "You should
have bet on her."

"Hmmmm, maybe I should have. She looks
pretty good from here," he joked. Then drop-

ping an arm around Caroline's slim shoulders he turned to her. He did it naturally without embarrassment and Caroline couldn't suppress the thrill of joy she felt. But that didn't make what she had to tell him any easier. In fact it was more difficult than she anticipated. She and Matt were getting more than their share of attention. The sidelong glances from Lisa and the twins were unmistakable. But why should that bother me? she asked herself.

"It's great you're free early today," Matt said interrupting her train of thought. "Are you ready to go? A group of us are going to try that new pizza place in the mall, so let's not keep everybody waiting."

"I can't." In retrospect Caroline realized she wasn't very tactful but she felt herself being swept away by Matt's enthusiasm and she had to stop it before it went too far.

"Can I speak to you for a moment, over here?" she asked quietly, and she walked to the other side of the hall away from all the inquisitive eyes.

An anxious crease appeared on Matt's brow as he followed her lead. "What's up?" he said questioningly as he leaned against a row of lockers.

"I can't see you tonight. I have a test Friday and I've got to study tonight," she blurted out.

"Well can't you do it later? We don't have many days like this you know," he said.

"I know. But I really can't see you tonight. I wouldn't be able to enjoy myself. I'd be too busy thinking about what I should be doing," she said.

"I see," he said. "Well, maybe I'll see you tomorrow. Give me a call tonight, *if you get a chance*," he added ironically. He smiled thinly.

"I will." Caroline touched his sleeve as he turned to rejoin his friends. She watched with mixed emotions as the group of students sauntered down the hallway to the exit. Matt's laughter rang out loudly and the girls' giggles filtered back to Caroline. She experienced a brief pang of regret. Or was it jealousy? Already, Matt seemed to have forgotten all about her.

In a last gesture of parting, she raised her hand to wave goodbye. But Matt didn't even turn around. In an instant he had disappeared from her sight.

7

Caroline and Beth spent nearly three hours reviewing geometry before calling it a night. They had covered a lot of territory and Caroline was pleased with the night's work.

Beth and Mrs. Anderson drove her home. She was tired and nervous. Just one more day and her geometry test would be over. That was all she could think about.

She hung her navy pea coat in the hall closet, and headed for her bedroom. She had just enough energy left to type the bibliography and footnotes for her term paper. Then she could sleep. "Caroline, is that you?" her mother called from the kitchen.

"It's me, mom." Caroline walked to the kitchen where she found her parents dressed in their pajamas, having a late night snack.

"Going to bed early I see," Caroline said from the doorway.

"No, not really, kiddo. There's a TV special on at ten. We just thought we'd get comfortable," her father grinned.

"And you," she said, scratching Amber behind an ear. "No wonder you didn't come running. Begging for a piece of chocolate cake, eh?"

"She's not going to get one," mother said. "It's not good for her teeth."

"But it's good for ours." Mr. Vickers winked as he poured two cups of coffee.

"She'll just have to settle for a dog biscuit." Mrs. Vickers placed a biscuit at Amber's feet. Amber devoured it instantly then stared at the box waiting for more.

"Where's Kurt?" Caroline tossed Amber another biscuit.

"He's at Linda Steiner's . . . studying, supposedly," her mother laughed. "He'll be home later. You've had a late day yourself, haven't you, honey? If basketball is going to cut into your studying time like this, I think we'll have to re-evaluate this situation."

"It wasn't practice, mom. I've been studying."

"With Matt?" Mrs. Vickers asked with a knowing smile. "Why didn't he stop in?"

Sitting on her father's knee, Caroline pilfered some of his cake. "It wasn't with Matt, mom. I've been with Beth. She's helping me with my geometry homework," she said between mouthfuls.

"Oh." Her mother sounded disappointed. "Didn't he give you a ride home?"

"Mom," Caroline explained patiently, "I wasn't with Matt. I don't expect him to be my chauffeur."

"That's absolutely right. I don't want my daughter using men for her own unscrupulous ends," Mr. Vickers laughed.

"I guess that wouldn't be nice," Mrs. Vickers reconsidered. "You've just started seeing him after all. It takes time to train them," her mother said, stealing a glance at her husband.

"I refuse to rise to the bait," he said in mock seriousness.

And so do I, Caroline thought nervously. She hadn't had a lot of free time lately. She knew her mother was dying to question her about Matt. Mornings had been too busy and everyone had been underfoot, hurrying to get to work or school. And Matt's presence in the house the last two evenings had hindered any conversation between mother and daughter. And now she really had to get to her paper. Deliberately ignoring her mother's disappointed look, she gave both her parents a quick kiss and said goodnight.

"I'll be typing for a little while. I have to turn in my term paper tomorrow. I won't be up too late." She was out the kitchen before anything but goodnight could be said.

Her typing finished and her term paper placed in a smart-looking vinyl folder, Caroline finally could go to bed but her thoughts kept drifting back to her day. She had found the time she needed to catch up on her geometry assignments but she wondered if the price had been worth it. She couldn't put Matt out of her mind. And she didn't like the idea of him hanging out with the Scott twins and Lisa. They were juniors, his equals, both popular and attractive.

He could fall for any one of them, she thought with a frown. Karen Scott may be going with the captain of the football team now but she was known for collecting boyfriends like some people collect stamps. *But if I can't trust Matt, I'd be better off without him.* With that thought Caroline drifted off for another night of restless sleep.

Thursday morning's geometry class passed all too quickly. Mr. Jeffers had more material he wanted to cover prior to the quiz but he had promised the students earlier that he'd spend at least a half hour answering any questions they might have.

"As I glance out at this sea of faces," he began, as he erased the last problem off the blackboard, "I see that everyone is here today —for once. I would like to repeat, there will be no makeup test." A low moan rose up from the students. "If you have kept up on your work you should be prepared. And, if you're not prepared . . . well, you might as well get it over with."

"Now, are there any questions?" A thicket of hands shot up in the air.

Caroline picked up her pencil and carefully recorded every question and explanation that was given. By the end of class she had six pages of additional notes and she had even asked a question herself. She noticed that Mr. Jeffers had called on her right away, even though other students had their hands up before her. Mr. Jeffers explained the answer slowly and in detail. He's really trying to help me, Caroline thought and she smiled in gratitude. She just wished there had been more time to prepare for the quiz. But knowing she had one more evening to study with Beth gave her confidence and hope.

The rest of the day dragged. The most exciting class was history. When her name was called she walked proudly to Mr. Camp's desk and presented her paper. She had done her best and she was pleased when she saw Mr. Camp skimming her report. His interest in her work brightened an otherwise drab morning and she set off to lunch in a happy frame of mind.

Beth and Sheila were already in the cafeteria by the time she got there. Lunch time was spent discussing Sheila's performance during the tryouts the night before. Sheila was on pins and needles and couldn't eat a morsel.

"I thought they'd tell us who made it right away," she complained. "But we won't find out until tomorrow. Old lady Winter, the home ec. teacher, is the proctor for the cheerleaders and she wants everyone who tried out in her homeroom before first period." Sheila sighed and continued. "Ms. Winter and the principal will probably congratulate the winners and console the losers, I guess. I wish I could go into a coma until tomorrow. This is driving me crazy."

Caroline hated to admit it but in a way she was glad Sheila was upset. It took her mind off her own problems. She had been living, sleeping, and eating geometry for the past five days. It felt good to think about someone else for a change.

Before lunch ended Caroline and Beth made arrangements to meet later at the Adamses' after Caroline's basketball practice. The qualms she had had the night before were long forgotten. She would simply tell Matt she couldn't meet him that night. After all, she could see how much Beth had helped her and it was her last evening before the quiz. She would just tell Matt ahead of time, instead of waiting until the last minute as she had done before.

At the end of the last period, before she went to her locker, Caroline went to Matt's homeroom. The halls were full of jabbering students returning to their homerooms and Caroline felt awkward. She was a sophomore in junior territory and she felt she stuck out like a sore thumb. She was so caught up in her thoughts that she hadn't been aware of the admiring looks she was getting from some of the upperclassmen.

She had never really considered herself attractive. She was even unaware of her assets: her clear complexion with its natural rosiness that made a blusher unnecessary, her large, hazel eyes, her shoulder length, shining hair. Today her hair was swept back from her face by small tortoise combs placed an inch or so above the ear, leaving her small lobes with their tiny gold hoops clearly exposed. Her gray pleated corduroy jeans were topped with a green tartan plaid shirt and vest. A sliver of ribbon tied beneath her collar completed her dress. The look was attractive and classic.

She saw Matt almost at the instant he saw her. A puzzled look crossed his face before he smiled tentatively in greeting. The other students were so busy rushing to their homerooms Caroline was certain no one was paying attention.

"I wanted to talk to you about yesterday," Caroline began. "I'm sorry I messed up your arrangements. I should have told you about my plans earlier."

"Oh that's all right," he said. "Grades are important. I guess you worked kind of late," he added, changing the subject. "You didn't call."

Caroline shut her eyes and leaned back against a locker. "I'm sorry," she said, reaching out and touching his hand. "I was working . . . I just forgot."

"No problem," Matt said. "So what's planned for tonight?"

"That's why I stopped by." She glanced at her watch quickly. The homeroom bell would ring soon. "I'm going to study with Beth again tonight after practice. She's been a big help to me."

"Okay, that's fine," he said stiffly. He smiled at her, but the smile did not reach his eyes. "I'll be seeing you." The homeroom bell sounded. They both hesitated a heartbeat longer, but the appearance of Matt's homeroom teacher canceled any further conversation.

"You're late for homeroom, aren't you, young lady?" the teacher said gruffly.

"Yes, sir," Caroline stammered and hurried down the hall.

The afternoon's practice was not a strenuous one nor did it last as long as the day before. They went through the usual limbering-up exercises and ran through the warm-up drills too. But more time was spent learning routine plays because Coach Cooper wanted to see them used at the next practice. Time passed quickly and before Caroline realized it she was running her last laps around the gym before the coach called the girls together for their brief meeting.

Caroline loosened her shoelaces and removed her wristbands as she squatted on the floor alongside Valerie Davis and several other friends she had made on the team.

"I just wanted to remind you—if you had forgotten—to pick up your uniform before you leave."

"Well, all right," someone shouted and all the girls cheered.

"Okay, now calm down," Coach Cooper smiled at her team. "They've already been cleaned so just press them a bit and bring them back tomorrow."

"The guys don't have to press their uniforms," a disgruntled voice yelled.

"Yeah," came another response.

"All right. Quiet down," the coach demanded. "We're not going to open that kettle of fish. We all know the situation here and at every other school in the area. The only way to really change things is to have a successful season. That's why we have new uniforms this year. We had a better year than the boy's team last year and, by heaven, we will again this year. You just wait and see."

Coach Cooper should have been a preacher, Caroline thought. She certainly knew how to psych the girls up.

"I just want you to know that I'm proud of all of you," the coach continued her pep talk. "You're a team and I know you'll play like one tomorrow. I've decided to break with tradition this year and name the starting lineups today, instead of tomorrow. It was a difficult decision to make."

Caroline knew what her coach meant. The competition for positions on the JV and Varsity squads had been fierce this year and, if it had been left up to Caroline, she wouldn't have been able to choose the top five players easily either. Fortunately Coach Cooper would now put an end to all speculation.

"Before I read the names, there's one more thing; I expect everyone to be present for *both* the Varsity and JV games. We won't have a lot of fan support; so we must support each other."

All the girls nodded in agreement and the coach withdrew a piece of paper from her skirt pocket. "The starting Varsity lineup for tomorrow's scrimmage," Caroline crossed her fingers and hid them in her socks, ". . . Valerie Davis . . . Laraine Kimbriel . . . Peggy Crum . . . Nancy Thomas . . . and *Caroline Vickers*."

Caroline was grateful for all the time and effort Beth had spent coaching her; however, the evening's study had not gone as well as the previous night's work. There were two areas that not even Beth could explain and Caroline's state of mind wasn't helping her attention span. She was trying to concentrate on math but every so often thoughts of Matt would distract her. She had missed him these last few days. She knew his feelings were hurt and she wanted to make it up to him as quickly as possible.

It was a long weary evening for both girls but even longer for Caroline who returned to her home to study a few hours more, stopping just long enough to eat warmed-up meatloaf.

The next day Caroline felt that she would have been better going directly to bed instead of cramming all night. She was so tired that she barely made it to homeroom before the warning bell sounded. While other students hurried off to their first period classes, Caroline had to rush to her locker, deposit her coat, and gather the texts and notebooks she needed for her morning classes.

As she rummaged around in her locker, the only thing Caroline could think about was how she wished Mr. Jeffers would cancel the math quiz! Perhaps the xerox machine would miraculously break down? Her stomach felt taunt and nervous. She slammed her locker closed, locked it securely, and sped down the hall to geometry class, nearly plowing into one or two students along the way.

"Hey, slow down," a familiar voice spoke behind her. Strong fingers clasped Caroline's elbow pulling her to a halt. Pivoting about in surprise Caroline found herself facing Matt.

"Where's the fire?"

"In Mr. Jeffers's geometry class, and if I don't hurry I'll be late."

"We wouldn't want that to happen, would we?" Matt smiled. He took her hand casually and escorted her down the hall.

"I'm glad I ran into you," he whispered in her ear. "I have a surprise for you."

Caroline beamed. "Well, don't keep me in suspense. Tell me." Though she had only been with him for a few minutes she already felt lighthearted and gay. Matt appeared happy too. Nothing seemed more important to Caroline at the moment than Matt's warm smile.

"Well, what is it?" she pressed again.

Slipping his hand into the back pocket of his jeans, Matt withdrew two blue tickets and waved them in the air.

"You're looking at the proud owner of two tickets to the biggest rock and roll concert of the year. There will be at least seven big name groups playing at the Meadowlands. Would you like to come with me?"

"Fantastic," Caroline exclaimed, "when is it?"

"When is it? Where have you been, lady? All the FM stations have been hyping the concert. It's tonight at eight."

The boisterous noise from the students around her dulled to a faint hum in Caroline's ear as a sweeping sense of dread washed over her. "I can't, Matt. I'd love to go if it were any other night but tonight. We have our first scrimmage of the year tonight and I'm one of the starters for Varsity. I can't skip out. You understand, don't you?"

Matt and Caroline were now blocking the doorway and annoyed students were forced to walk around them. Matt snapped his fingers. "Well, you play the first game, right? By the time your game is over and you change . . . we would only be forty-five minutes late."

"No . . . we'd be later than that," she explained softly. "I really would love to go but I have to stay for the JV game too. Just go without me and have a good time," she said sadly.

"Darn, it, Caroline." Matt was angry now. "It always seems to be something . . ."

"I know," she said rapidly as the first period bell rang. "The last few days haven't been my best. But it will get better, I promise. We still have our weekends. I really must go now," she said hurriedly. "Stop by and see me before my game, okay?" she called as she ran to her class.

8

Pulling her hair back into a ponytail, Caroline tied an emerald green ribbon around it in a sporty bow. The bow nearly matched the color of her uniform, a solid green sleeveless top and shorts with the words "Glendale Chargers" and number 44 printed in gold letters across the front and back.

She closed her gym locker and went looking for Valerie. She needed her friend's calming influence. The excitement in the locker room was too much for her. She especially wanted to play well. If she did, she was certain her starting position on the Varsity Squad would be assured for the opening game of the season next week.

Caroline found Valerie dressed for the game sitting alone on a bench in the middle of a row of lockers. Her closed eyes and rapid breathing alerted Caroline at once that something was wrong.

"Hey, are you okay?" she asked and waited patiently until her friend smiled in reply.

"Oh sure. It's just a case of nerves," Valerie said shakily. "I'll be fine once the game starts."

"Phew. That's good. You had me worried there for a second. I know how you feel." Caroline sat on the bench facing her friend. "I'm the same way. I usually forget about it too once I start playing. It's funny, but you don't strike me as the type to get nervous before a game. You always look so confident. So self-assured. It's kind of comforting to know I'm not the only one who goes through this."

"Believe me you're not," Valerie chuckled as she rose from the bench. "Let's go warm up and take our minds off it. We're due to start pretty soon anyway."

Leading the way past other team players in various stages of undress, Valerie approached a group about to enter the gym when Beth and Sheila came running up to join them.

"Hi, you two!" Beth said hugging Caroline

then smiling at Val in turn. "We just stopped by to wish you luck."

"And deliver a message," Sheila said breathlessly. "Matt's outside. He'd like to see you for a minute, *if* you can find the time," she teased.

Caroline spotted Matt a few feet away watching the visiting team warm up. His profile was just as pleasant to look at as the rest of him and for a few seconds Caroline stood silently and admired him before making her presence known.

"Hi," she said as she stepped up to him.

"Hi yourself," Matt said amiably. "How did your quiz go today?"

"Oh great!" Caroline answered a bit too quickly to her own ears. "I'm sure I did well," she added enthusiastically; but that wasn't quite true. She wasn't sure of anything these days, least of all her performance on her quiz.

Caroline had arrived at her geometry class just as Mr. Jeffers was beginning to hand out the test papers. Her lateness for homeroom and her rushed confrontation with Matt had left her totally frazzled and off balance. It had definitely not been the right frame of mind to take a test. But it was all over now. She had done the best she could. There was nothing to do but wait for the final results to come in. It had been her problem, not Matt's. After denying him so much of her time she wasn't about to cry on his shoulder and spoil his evening further.

"That's good. I'm glad to hear it," he smiled. "I just came by to wish you luck. I hope you have a good game tonight."

"Thanks." She smiled. She knew how proud Matt was and the effort it had cost him to come to congratulate her. "I hope you have a good time at the concert. I've heard some of the students talking about it. Well more than some," she laughed. "It looks like the whole school is going. It really should be fun."

"Yes I know. That's why I wanted you to come with me," Matt said. The conversation was taking a direction Caroline wanted to avoid.

"I know you wanted me to go with you. And I really wish I could. But look at it this way. There will be other concerts to go to. You'll see."

"Is that supposed to make me feel better?" His tone was angry. "I'm sorry," he said quickly. "I didn't mean to say that. I apologize. Forgive me?"

"That's okay, really. I guess that *was* a pretty patronizing remark. I only wanted to make you feel better. I'm sorry about that extra ticket you bought," she hurriedly continued. "Have you been able to sell it yet?"

"No. But I haven't really tried. A group of us are going to the concert together, so if someone needs a ticket they can have it. Or else I may try selling it once we get there." He shrugged.

"Well, I hope you get your money back. It would kind of make up for things—a little," Caroline murmured regretfully.

In a playful gesture belying the seriousness of the last minutes, Matt flipped Caroline's ponytail and set it swinging.

"Nothing can make up for the fact you can't come with me tonight," he said. "But since there's nothing we can do about tonight . . . how about meeting me at the stables tomorrow for a ride?"

"I'll be there."

"Bright and early?"

"Bright and early," she smiled. "And that's a promise."

Although Caroline was tired from her night-owl hours of the previous nights, her on-court performance didn't show it. Her outside jumpshot was on target and her defense was unshakable as she tallied a total of fifteen points for the game.

The tempo of the Varsity scrimmage was brisk from the opening tip-off, resembling a season finale rather than the season opener it was. Coach Cooper liberally substituted players throughout the game in order to pinpoint the best combination of players but it was apparent from the outset that her starting lineup was the best. Caroline and Valerie played together as if they had been doing so for years instead of a couple of weeks. The entire starting Charger quintet played with such precision that even with the substitutions by the end of the fourth quarter the Varsity team was victorious by eleven points. Unfortunately, the JV team did not fare as well. They lost their scrimmage by six points but Caroline, Beth, Sheila, and Val had a wonderful time cheering them on.

The evening concluded at the Vickers homestead with the foursome enjoying hot cider, popcorn, and much laughter in the coziness of the glass-enclosed porch. The girls could look up at the stars or watch the rustling trees in the chilly wind, as the fire Mr. Vickers built crackled before them.

The companionship Caroline felt with her friends was even more warming than the snapping fire. Not only was she celebrating the first of what she was certain would be many Charger victories, she was doing it with the people she cared about most.

However, in spite of all the good feelings and fun they were having, Caroline thought how much better the evening would have been if Matt had been there too. She imagined the firelight shimmering off his dark locks and the reddish glow of the flames dancing on his face as he stared into it. She could picture those intent blue eyes beckoning her toward him. In seconds, she would find herself enveloped in his arms. And just before the fiery embers flickered their last, he'd tenderly cradle her face and kiss her, murmuring the words she longed to hear. *Oh Matt. How I wish you were here.* Absentmindedly, Caroline crumpled her napkin and threw it into the flames. She watched it shrivel and grow black. The charred remains flew up the chimney. Would this happen also to her daydreams?

Caroline met Matt as promised and with her parents' approval, once she told them where she was off to so early in the morning. Mr. Vickers finished his coffee and smiled quietly as he watched his wife nearly push Caroline out the door. For once, Caroline didn't fight her mother. She was as much in a hurry to see Matt as her mother was for her to see him. It was going to be a wonderful day, she could feel it. Her parents had been satisfied with her answer that she thought she had done well on her quiz. They were happy about her friendship with Matt. On a day like today nothing could go wrong, she thought.

She arrived at the stables just as Matt was going on his mid-morning break. For half an hour she had him all to herself as they rode across the grounds at breakneck speed.

Later, when she arrived home, her parents were not surprised to hear that Matt had asked her out to the movies for Sunday. The latest space war saga was playing locally and he wanted to see it—with her. The rest of Saturday and Sunday passed slowly as she waited for evening to arrive.

When the hour finally came, Caroline happily answered the door to let Matt in. As they walked into the living room where her parents were reading the paper, she was struck by how different this date was from their first. There were no evasions or sneaking around this time. All that was behind her now.

Just as Matt and Caroline were about to leave, Kurt came running down the stairs. He had a date too—for the same movie. And Mr. Vickers slyly suggested they all go together.

"Take the wagon. It'll be more comfortable for four than either of the cars you guys drive," he laughed.

It was a first to be sure; but Kurt and Matt were all for it so who was Caroline to complain? She did feel a little funny at first when Matt opened doors for her or helped her across the street. She thought Kurt would start laughing any second, until she realized he was doing the same for his date. As the evening progressed, Caroline felt perfectly comfortable holding Matt's hand or walking with her arm around his waist with her brother there. The arguments and disappointments she and Matt had in the past few days now seemed unimportant and childish.

Later, snuggled warmly in her bed with Amber contentedly by her side, Caroline wondered how she could ever have doubted Matt's love. They were meant for each other. She just knew it. And she couldn't wait to see him again.

9

Caroline awoke the next morning, with more energy than she had felt in a long time. Just wanting to get out of bed was quite a feat in itself for a Monday. Now she couldn't even wait to get to school! Matt was on her mind. They had had such a wonderful time the night before. She wished she had invited him to the Sadie Hawkins Dance. She had wanted to ask him several times but they hadn't been alone long enough for her to do it. The big event was still several days away.

Her desire to get to school was not solely

spurred by thoughts of seeing Matt, although their plans to meet after basketball practice weren't exactly a deterrent. For some inexplicable reason, Caroline felt terrific. She felt she could do anything and everything. Life was wonderful and she was eager to start the day.

Bounding out of bed, Caroline peered out her window. Overnight the weather had taken a drastically cold turn, ending once and for all dreams of a late Indian summer. After a fast shower she pulled on a pair of navy blue textured stockings and her black boots. Searching through her closet she found her favorite jean skirt and topped everything off with the cream cableknit turtleneck she had bought earlier in the year. Before leaving the room she slipped in a pair of gold hoop earrings, sprayed herself with a little Charlie perfume, and smoothed on a pale plum lip gloss. Her morning toilette was more extensive these days, now that Matt had entered her life. Finally, she was finished. One more lick with her hair brush and she was on her way.

"You should eat something," Mrs. Vickers yelled as Caroline ran for the door.

"Don't worry, I won't starve between now and lunch," she called as she grabbed her things. "If I get hungry I'll munch on an apple between classes," and out the door she went.

Her boundless energy and high spirits made the trip to school pass quickly. They carried her through her homeroom and even lasted into geometry class. She slid into her seat just as a grim-faced Mr. Jeffers was placing his briefcase on his desk. He didn't look up when she came in, nor did he check her name in the attendance book. With a sharp click, he opened the briefcase and placed a stack of papers in front of him. There was an ominous pause as he gazed coldly at his class. Finally he spoke.

"I was debating whether to hand back your papers today or tomorrow. Quite frankly, I was disappointed in a number of people's grades."

Caroline shifted nervously in her seat. Mr. Jeffer's eyes seemed to bore right through her to an unknown spot on the back wall.

"I wasn't in the right frame of mind to discuss your quiz last week, and I'm still not, but there's no point in dragging it out. . . . I'm asking some of you to see me as soon as possible. . . . You'll find a note on the bottom right-hand corner."

Stepping away from his desk, Mr. Jeffers began to hand out the papers. Caroline did not dare look up and pretended to be very absorbed in doodling in her assignment book.

Talking all the while Mr. Jeffers continued handing out the papers in a distracting ritual that everyone had to sit through. He never called the student's name. Instead, he casually walked about the room passing out the papers and talking about the test and the general class performance. A student would be sitting anxiously expecting his test to be dropped on his desk any second and it wouldn't happen. Next thing he knew, Mr. Jeffers would be leaning across another desk and tapping him on the head with it or coming up behind him to slip it across his shoulder.

None of these approaches, however, were used on Caroline. Mr. Jeffers took his time walking down her aisle handing out one or two papers along the way. As he stood opposite her desk he reached across to hand a paper to another student before placing hers in front of her, face down on her desk. Mr. Jeffers was always careful to hold everyone's paper in such a way that no one could mistakenly see anyone else's grade; but Caroline felt everyone saw hers, and her face flushed hotly.

Don't be so paranoid, she berated herself. You didn't even see your grade, so how could anyone else see it? Stop being silly and get on with it. She took a deep breath and turned her paper over. This is impossible! There must be some mistake. I know I didn't do that badly, she thought. D minus!

Caroline's body flashed hot then cold. She stared down at her paper. It was all she could do to keep from crying. Next to losing Matt this was the worst thing that could have happened to her and she dreaded telling her parents. They'll want me to quit basketball, I know it, she thought. This grade has got to be a mistake. It's just got to.

"I'm having office hours during your free period today and during your lunch hour," Mr. Jeffers told his students. "I'll contact your lunch proctors and let them know I'll be in my homeroom if some of you wish to cut your lunch short and see me. I'll also have office hours after school for as long as needed. Those of you who should see me, don't wait. See me today."

Caroline didn't know how she made it through the rest of her morning classes. She sat at her desks, books opened and ready, but nothing was sinking in. Her notebook pages remained blank and she'd have quite a time later getting the information she missed. But what did a few missed pages of notes matter now?

Coming upon Mr. Jeffers's homeroom Caroline hoped she had beaten out other students who had been asked to see him. Luck was with her. She found her teacher alone and looking out the classroom window. Caroline knocked timidly on the door and entered with apprehension.

Mr. Jeffers's smile was warm and reassuring as he turned and walked over to his desk, taking a seat on its edge. "It's really cold out there," he said, in a vain attempt to make Caroline comfortable. "If this keeps up there will be some awfully cold weather greeting the trick-or-treaters this Friday," he laughed. "But you didn't come here to talk about that, did you, Caroline? What happened? I thought you had everything under control?"

"I did," Caroline said emphatically. "There's got to be some mistake, Mr. Jeffers," Caroline said thrusting her paper into his hand. "I know this stuff. I mean I know the work," she corrected herself. "I studied it. I even had a friend help me. Could you please check my test again?"

Shaking his head slowly from side to side Mr. Jeffers barely looked at the test paper before putting it down.

"I've already checked it twice. I gave you every break I could, Caroline. There's no mistake. You obviously just weren't concentrating. Here, let me show you," he said and pointed out a problem. "You started out on the right track, then you made a silly mistake. You did that on a couple of problems."

"But *I know*, I know this material," Caroline replied hastily. "Really I do."

"Okay, Caroline," Mr. Jeffers sighed. "Let's go over the quiz together and you show me."

For the next thirty minutes or so Caroline and Mr. Jeffers reviewed her quiz. With pencil in hand Caroline went through the problems one at a time. Aside from one or two questions from her teacher Caroline did all the talking.

Sitting back in his chair, Mr. Jeffers looked at Caroline in disbelief. "Why didn't you do that last Friday?" he questioned. "That's at least C work, almost worthy of a C plus."

"I don't know," Caroline said wearily. "The day just started out all wrong. I stayed up so late the night before studying. I overslept the next day and I was late getting to school. Then a . . . a friend stopped me in the hallway and insisted on talking to me," she finished lamely. *Now why did I say that?* Caroline was mortified and would have gladly bitten off her tongue if she could only take back those words. She didn't mean to tell Mr. Jeffers *everything* but once she got started she couldn't stop. She hated making excuses for herself—that was tacky enough. But blaming it on someone else, especially Matt, was worse. She waited for a lecture from Mr.

Jeffers on taking responsibility for one's own actions. But wasn't it Matt's fault, at least a little? I may have been running late that morning but talking to him really threw me off kilter. Maybe I would have done better if he hadn't upset me about that concert. Mr. Jeffers knows I can do the work. I just proved that, didn't I?

Mr. Jeffers showed no reaction to Caroline's accounting of that morning. He listened and smiled which embarrassed Caroline even more. He didn't launch into the lecture she grimly expected.

"I do remember you coming in late that morning; I noticed you took a while before starting," he said. "It's obvious you have at least an average if not slightly better than average grasp of the material, Caroline."

"So you'll change my grade," she said anxiously.

"No, Caroline. I'm sorry I can't," Mr. Jeffers stated with genuine sincerity. "I'd like to, but if I did it for you I'd have to do it for everyone who came in here. Who's to say that under different circumstances all those who failed or did poorly would pass with flying colors while those who passed admirably would fail," he reasoned. "No, I can't change your grade. The D minus must stand along with the D grade which is now your class average."

"My class average is a D!" Caroline nearly yelled.

"I'm afraid so," Mr. Jeffers nodded. "This grade *really* hurt you, young lady."

That was the understatement of the year, and Caroline couldn't believe it. This was a blow she hadn't remotely considered; she was too busy convincing herself her grade would be changed. Now there was no hope of that at all! "Mom and dad will have a fit," she groaned. "I'll be off the team now, for sure."

Caroline was too occupied with agonizing over her predicament to notice Mr. Jeffers pick up both tests and compare them once more.

"Don't look so glum," he finally said cheerfully. "Let's not throw in the towel so soon. I realize you have a lot at stake, not only my course but as a member of one of Glendale's athletic teams. If you fail this course you could be off the team too. However, I think you can make a comeback if you're really willing to work."

"Oh, I am, Mr. Jeffers," Caroline replied.

"Good. The final for this quarter is in a few weeks. If you get a C on the final I'll give you a C for the quarter. You can still come out on top on this, but it is up to you. Once a student hits that D level it's so easy to slip that one notch more to an F. And in this case, since the final covers everything we've studied thus far, it'll be that much harder. But if you want to pass, you can do it. I'll get you a tutor and I'll personally help you any way I can. Well, what do you say?"

Caroline's head was spinning by the time she left Mr. Jeffers's homeroom. The grades would stand as they were. She'd have to tell her parents the bad news. And now she had a tutor to contend with! She had to prove to Mr. Jeffers she wanted to pass. This time she had seen the wisdom in accepting his help. Money wouldn't be a problem. She knew her parents would want her to have as much help as she needed. And though Beth had been wonderful she had a few problems with geometry herself. There really wasn't any choice. She was caught between the proverbial rock and a hard place. There was no way out.

She went to basketball practice as usual but her heart wasn't in it. She went through the motions of the drills but the all-consuming magic wasn't there. She couldn't forget the mess she had managed to get herself into. All she could think about was telling her parents.

By the time Matt arrived, she was in no mood for his company. And when he accused her of not paying attention to him, she seized the opportunity to beg off by complaining of an upset stomach. As much as she dreaded the prospect she had to talk to her parents right away.

Dinner was almost on the table by the time Caroline got home. The table was set, the salad ready, the lasagna, a favorite of hers, needed only a few minutes more before the family could sit down to eat.

In her state of anxiety Caroline knew she couldn't sit through a meal without talking to her parents first. She was getting so upset she really was getting sick.

Collecting her test papers and the small note Mr. Jeffers had written in her behalf, Caroline went in search of her parents. She found them in the kitchen. Mr. Jeffers's note said it all. ". . . I'm very optimistic about Caroline's future performance. Although she is still having a little trouble I'm confident she can pass this course," he had written. "Students sometimes 'freeze' during a test and I think that's what happened to her. However, to help her over those remaining rough spots, I have obtained a tutor for her . . ."

Caroline knew the note by heart. All she could do was sit quietly as her parents read it for themselves and looked over her test work.

"Well that's it, Ted," Mrs. Vickers sighed. "As far as I'm concerned this is it. No more basketball. Obviously, Caroline can't play basketball and devote the time she needs for geometry too. She'll just have to quit the team. That's all."

Although Mr. Vickers was slower to react, he echoed his wife's sentiments. "This definitely *isn't* what we expected," he said slowly. "Especially since you told us you did okay. This is not okay. Maybe you are overtaxing yourself, honey. Basketball and geometry just seems to be a combination that's too much for you. I think it would be better if you did drop basketball as your mother said. I wish there were another way," he added. Caroline knew her father felt as badly as she did. Her athletic successes were a source of intense pride to him.

"It's not like I didn't try," she said. "You know Beth was helping me."

"Yes, we know that. You were working hard. Your mother and I could both see that. You put in some long hours."

"But it wasn't enough, Caroline. You still got a D," Mrs. Vickers cut in.

"I know and believe me, I was just as surprised as you were. But even Mr. Jeffers admits I know more than I showed in that test," she said. "He said so in that note. I was just nervous. I know I'll do better on the final."

"We're sure you will, baby. Without basketball you'll have plenty of time to study. It's just taking up too much of your time,"

Mrs. Vickers told her daughter. "Now let's eat."

"Wait a minute. Please," Caroline protested. "I don't see how you can say that. Basketball doesn't take up any more of my time than field hockey did. Or Matt does for that matter," she said.

"Oh, Caroline. There's no comparison between the time spent on basketball and with Matt," her mother laughed. "Besides, every girl needs a boyfriend! Boyfriends are a necessity in high school. You can't have much of a social life without them. Unless you want to spend all your time with the girls."

"Well there's nothing wrong with that, mom. Girls are as much fun to be with as guys," Caroline said, though she couldn't imagine her life without having Matt to look forward to. "Anyway, whether it's Matt, or basketball, they still take time away from my studies. But that's not the point. I did my best," she said looking from one frowning parent to the other. "Yes, I didn't do well on the test," she conceded. "But I didn't out and out fail it either. I proved to Mr. Jeffers I know more than I showed in that quiz. It's all in his note," she emphasized. "I had five days to pull things together; but it wasn't enough. I just don't think it's fair to penalize me like this. I can still play basketball until I fail the course—which I won't," she was quick to say.

"I should be allowed to play. I think I deserve a little more time."

The silence following Caroline's words was more deafening than a sudden clap of thunder on a sultry summer evening. Faced with such determination, her parents were at a loss for words.

After glancing through her teacher's note once more Mr. Vickers walked over to his wife who now was putting dinner on the dining room table. They whispered intently together while Caroline agonizingly awaited the verdict.

"Okay, kiddo," Mr. Vickers smiled as he and her mother returned to the kitchen. "Your mom and I agree, maybe five days wasn't enough time." For the first time Caroline felt there was a ray of hope. "However, something has to be done about your grade. You need more time to study, that's obvious. The tutor Mr. Jeffers is getting you is going to be a great help. Perhaps that's all you need. Someone who really knows this stuff. How often did you plan on seeing him anyway?"

"I thought I'd see him twice a week, after basketball practice," Caroline said eagerly.

"That's good. We think twice a week will be fine; but not after basketball practice," her father slipped in.

"We're sure you can make some arrangement with your coach to free you from prac-

tice twice a week for the sake of your studies,"
Mrs. Vickers said. "You can't be fresh and
alert after basketball to put in a couple of
hours with a tutor. And I'm sure your tutor
wouldn't want to be bothered after basketball
to tutor you anyway. You'd be tying up his
evening," she reasoned.

"But I can't cut basketball practice," Caroline cried. "I'm a starter. How would that
look?"

"We don't care how it looks, Carrie," her
father said firmly. "We only care about your
grades."

"But Dad . . ."

"No buts, Caroline, and that's not all. A D
may be passing and acceptable but it's not
acceptable to me or your mother. If you fail
that final in four weeks or get a D again, that's
it. Your basketball season is over."

"But I can still play with a D grade."

"Maybe the school says so," Mrs. Vickers
said, "but we don't. Besides, if you plan to go
to college you don't want a D on your academic report, do you?"

"I plan on going to college, but my grades
won't matter that much," Caroline insisted.
"I'm going on an athletic scholarship. You
know State's interested already. My grades
aren't that important."

"Grades are always important, Caroline,"
her father said firmly. "How many athletes

have you read about who went to school on an athletic scholarship, injured themselves, were unable to play, and were thrown out because their grades couldn't cut it? If you don't develop good study habits now, who's to say it won't happen to you . . . but let's not put the cart before the horse," he said more gently. "There's interest at State but that's two years away and anything can happen in that time."

"Who knows? Two years from now you might not even want to play sports anymore," her mother interrupted.

"That'll never happen."

"Be that as it may," her father said. "This is the deal. Two days a week—no basketball. And a C or better on your final or basketball is definitely out for the remainder of the year. We're sorry if this sounds unreasonable to you," Mr. Vickers said rising from the table, "but it's for your own good. If you won't think about your future and prepare for it on your own, we'll do it for you. Now, let's eat. I'm starved."

10

Anything that can go wrong will go wrong. It was Murphy's Law and for Caroline a prophetic description of her present situation.

Instead of attending a practice which was crucial preparation for the basketball team's upcoming "official" opener on Friday, Caroline sat in the school library awaiting the arrival of her new tutor—David Gleason.

A senior and president of the National Honor Society, David was one of Glendale's resident "brains." Ranked number two in his class, he was sure to be the Salutatorian at this year's commencement exercises and, according to Mr. Jeffers, he was one of the best tutors. "He's always obtained excellent results," Mr. Jeffers had said to her after class that morning, "and his rates are very reasonable. If you put in half the effort that David will, you'll pass the final with ease."

Caroline sincerely hoped Mr. Jeffers wasn't giving her the standard pep talk reserved for every student in trouble. The next few weeks were going to be tough ones. She didn't kid herself on that score. She would be accountable for her tutorial time to her parents. They wanted to see all her homework and extra work assignments. Plus Mr. Jeffers would surely be watching her classroom progress more closely too. And of course, now she had a tutor to juggle in an already busy schedule.

No one needed to be a mind reader to know that something was on Caroline's mind as she walked into the locker room. Her steps were slow and precise. She didn't stop to suit up for practice but headed directly for the coach's office.

With more confidence than she felt Caroline sat down and came to the heart of the matter at once. She explained the hapless events leading up to her situation and her parents' irrevocable decision. There would be no basketball for her for two days a week. It was either that or hang up her sneakers. There were no two ways about it. Yet making it sound as though it were not the end of the world but rather an unfortunate temporary situation, called for some acting ability she wasn't sure she could muster.

It was fifteen minutes of sheer torture, but she managed to paint a determined smile on her face. Luckily, the tears that threatened to cloud her vision remained in hiding.

"I really am sorry about your troubles, Caroline, but if you need the time by all means take it. I told you once that basketball wasn't everything," the coach said. "I'm glad you want to stick this out and stay on the team. I'm sure you'll be back on top of your math work in no time. However," she continued sadly, "you realize this will affect the starting lineup for Friday's game."

That was just like Coach Cooper. While other coaches would do almost anything to win, she followed her own drummer. If an athlete didn't deserve to play because she didn't or couldn't put forth the time and effort needed, she didn't play. Unlike the male coaches, ability alone wasn't the determining factor of who played and who sat on the bench. There were no prima donnas on Coach Cooper's teams. There were only rules and everyone was to follow them. No one was indispensable. That was always the way she ran her teams . . . unfortunately for Caroline.

Ignoring the questioning looks from her fellow teammates, Caroline had quickly left the locker room for her meeting with David Gleason. Now alone, with only her thoughts for company, she couldn't decide what was the more terrible, not being able to play basketball for two days a week, not being a starter anymore, or having to explain her twice-weekly absences to her teammates.

What a mess. If only I had studied harder for that quiz, I wouldn't be in this jam now. But there was no use thinking of what might have been. There was nothing left to do but live with the situation, until she redeemed herself. All her energy was needed to do that. There wasn't time to feel sorry for herself too.

Caroline fidgeted in her stiff-backed wooden chair, her gaze pinned to the library door. *If I have to see a tutor we can at least start on time, for heaven's sake,* she thought grumpily. Then reluctantly, to occupy herself until David's arrival, she pulled out another homework assignment and went to it. There would be more than one final at the end of these weeks. She didn't want to complicate matters by having her grades slip in another subject.

Pressure, pressure, pressure. Any more and I'm going to explode, she thought near panic. Then taking hold of herself she began to work. How much time passed as she tackled her biology notes Caroline wasn't sure.

Her concentration was disrupted when a noisy group of students rustled the silence of the room. Books were unceremoniously thrown into the return bin and tables filled up with whispering students more bent on socializing, it seemed, than studying. Caroline recognized one of the Scott twins as a major offender. Whether it was Karen or Sharon, like everyone except their closest pals, she couldn't tell and really didn't care. It was only David Gleason's presence she was interested in and he was already twenty minutes late. But just as she had decided to leave, the library door swung open and in he strode. He paused by the doorway till he had included her in his sweeping glance. His loping stride covered the distance between them. His almond brown eyes were nearly hidden behind gold-rimmed glasses that seemed to sit slightly off center on a nose more ample than most. When he smiled, he revealed a tiny gap between two front teeth. Instinctively Caroline found herself comparing him to Matt.

"Hi," he said smoothly as he slid in the seat across from her. "I'm sorry I'm late but I got caught up in something else." I suppose that makes it all right, Caroline thought, annoyed by this stranger who held her athletic future so carelessly in his hands.

As if reading her thought David smiled apologetically and said, "Don't worry. I won't make a habit out of being late. I owe you some time, okay?"

His attitude was a little cocky but his smile was infectious. Despite her earlier anger Caroline relaxed a little.

"See. I knew I could get you to smile! We don't want to start off on the wrong foot now, do we? Now . . ." he said, suddenly all business, "we won't do anything strenuous today. I just wanted to meet you and discuss your problems as you see them. I've already talked to Mr. Jeffers and I know his opinion. But I'm really interested in yours. . . ."

As much as Caroline tried, her mind wandered, making it difficult to hold onto David's words. The giggles and whispers of some students and the comings and goings of others distracted her. She felt as though everyone were eavesdropping even though they were sitting apart from the rest. More than once her eyes met the inquisitive look of another student. Twice she found the ardent gaze of a twin glued to their table. She was beginning to feel like a mannequin on display. Who could be expected to concentrate like this?

"Well? What do you feel your main problem is?" David finished.

Embarrassed, Caroline blushed. The last

few moments had been lost on her. If she didn't get herself together, she could well imagine the report David would give Mr. Jeffers if he asked.

"I'm sorry," Caroline said snapping her mind back to attention. "What did you say?" she asked meekly.

"I said," he stressed, "do you have trouble approaching the problems themselves or are the rules still a little cloudy?"

"Yes."

"Yes to what?" he asked, the humor glinting in his eyes.

"Yes, I do have a problem with some of the rules. And sometimes I am stumped on how to attack a problem. It really depends on the problem," she responded irritably.

Puzzled, David surveyed his new pupil. He noted the tension in her wandering eyes. "This isn't working out too well for you, is it?"

"No, I guess not. It's just so . . . so distracting in here."

"Would you rather go someplace else?"

Caroline nodded.

"Okay. I really think a person should be tutored in an atmosphere where she'll be the most comfortable, anyway. We can go someplace else. Then we'll look over all your tests to date," he said beginning to rise.

"Oh no," Caroline laughed at herself. "I certainly am making a fiasco of our first meeting. I only brought my last quiz. The other tests are at home."

"Relax. That's no problem. Glendale isn't *that* big," David smiled and picked up her books with his own. "I have a car outside. We can go to your place and work or we can pick up your papers and go to the town library, or my place for that matter. Both my folks work so they won't be home for another couple of hours yet," he smiled. "Whatever you want to do, babe, is fine with me."

Pocketing her change, Caroline picked up her tray and ambled back to the lunch table where Beth and Sheila were already devouring their lunches.

"Really, Beth. I don't see how you can eat this pudding. It looks like brown glop to me. I feel guilty buying it for you," Caroline said, sliding the dessert over to her friend.

"Just the sight of it is enough to make me throw up," Sheila agreed, "but you know Beth. She can eat anything."

"And does," Caroline laughed.

"*If* you don't mind," Beth said with a playfully haughty air. "I'd rather you not discuss my eating habits with such disdain."

"Well, don't keep us in suspense," Sheila prodded. "How did basketball practice go yesterday?"

"Yeah. Did anyone ask you where you were on Tuesday?" Beth asked.

"Practice went fine," Caroline said as she sipped her soup. "And no. No one said anything, but I was only gone for one day. I'm sure there will be a lot of tongues wagging after today when I don't show up for practice. And if I don't start tomorrow against River-side you can bet there will be *a lot* of talk."

"Oh, Caroline. I really feel bad for you," Sheila sympathized. "Won't your parents change their minds? Maybe David wouldn't mind tutoring you after practice."

"No way. I've tried talking to them. They've made their decision and they won't change it," Caroline said.

"Well. I guess that's that," Beth said breezily. "By the way," she said, "what does Matt think about your new tutor? David isn't exactly ugly, you know. Actually he's really rather cute."

"I know what you mean," Sheila sighed wistfully. "Brains and beauty all in one nice package and now he's free. Some people have all the luck."

"Believe me, I don't consider myself lucky. This whole thing is just awful. David's nice enough but I'd gladly not see him at all if I could get around it," Caroline moaned.

"Well! What does Matt say?" Beth pushed.

"Matt doesn't say anything. I mean he

doesn't know," she said to two pairs of suggestively arched eyebrows. "It's not what you think. I've tried to talk to him about what's been happening with me. Boy is he going to think I'm a dope," she sighed. "I called him yesterday evening after practice, and I called him after David left on Tuesday, but he hasn't returned my calls yet."

"Woa. Wait a minute," Sheila pounced. "Not so fast. Back up. You said David left. David left where?"

"Left my house, ninny. I forgot the test we were going to discuss so he offered to drive me home and get it," Caroline clarified. "Then since nobody was home yet and the place was quiet, we decided to work there. It worked out pretty well too."

"Oh. I see," her friends giggled in unison.

"No. You don't. Don't be so wise, you two. It was all on the up and up. Besides, it gave my parents a chance to meet him. They are paying him, you know."

"True . . . true," Beth replied slowly. "It all sounds reasonable to me. And I'm sure it'll sound reasonable to Matt. When are you going to tell him?"

"It's not like I haven't tried. What's the big deal anyway?" Caroline was getting annoyed.

"It's no big deal. So when are you going to tell him?" Sheila asked.

"I just feel so stupid. I told him I did great

on that quiz," she groaned. "Now it's all backfiring in my face. If he doesn't call me tonight, I guess I'll just tell him when I see him. Now can we pick on one of you for a while?"

It was the end of the day and David met Caroline promptly after their homeroom period ended and headed for the school parking lot.

"See, I told you I wouldn't be late today."

"Well, it's nice to know you're a man of your word," Caroline said.

"Believe me. I try never to keep a pretty girl waiting." Caroline smiled knowingly. She knew enough about him now not to take him too seriously.

"You know he's smart but let me tell you the *good* stuff," Sheila had insisted before they left the cafeteria. "He was seeing Mary Evans for the longest time but they broke up a little while ago. David passes his time flirting with everything in a skirt, or tight-fitting jeans," she laughed. "But he's harmless. It's all a big cover-up. He was really hurt when she stopped seeing him. So don't take his kidding too seriously."

The warning wasn't necessary. Caroline had no intention of getting involved with anyone else. Matt was all she needed or wanted. David was just her tutor and in time maybe they would become good friends. But for now their relationship was strictly business, and she wanted to keep it that way.

"Well, have you decided where you want to work today?" Dave asked as they stopped in front of his car.

"Yes. I think we really got a lot done at my house the other day. My mother will probably be home but everyone else won't show up till about five or so. My dad will be working and that's Kurt's usual arrival time; so why don't we go back there?"

"That's fine with me. Maybe your mom still has more of those oatmeal raisin cookies?"

"Hmmm. Could be. Let's go and find out."

As Caroline settled into the front seat, she spotted Matt near the front carport and stuck her head out the window to wave. Huh. I thought he was looking right at me. I guess he can't see me, she thought.

"Can you wait just one more minute?" she asked David as he started the engine. "There's someone I want to talk to."

It was very cool for such an early afternoon. Not too many students were outside, Caroline could see, as she headed for Matt who seemed contented to stand and wait for her to reach him.

"Hi, stranger," Caroline grinned as she reached him. "I've been trying to reach you for the past two days. Didn't you get my messages?"

"Yes."

"Well," Caroline said, slightly confused. "I was hoping I'd hear from you by now."

"Why?" Matt asked. "So you can keep stringing me along?"

"What are you talking about?" Caroline cried above the ever increasing wind.

"I didn't believe it when people told me they saw you and Dave Gleason together," Matt said. "Then when I came by your homeroom this afternoon, who do I see leaving together? You didn't waste much time, did you! And I thought you were different! I also thought your basketball was so important to you, you wouldn't cut practice for anything. Or is it okay to cut practice when you have a *really good* reason?" he said jerking his head toward David's car.

He doesn't mean what he's saying, Caroline thought frantically. He just doesn't understand. He will when I explain.

More students were coming out of the building by this time and cars were pulling up to pick up students. Caroline lowered her voice. "I can explain," she whispered urgently. "If you'll just listen. Can't we go somewhere private and talk? Let me just go talk to David for a second."

"Do you think I'm that stupid?" Matt replied loudly. Heads turned in their direction. They were the center of attention. Then a feminine voice came out of nowhere; Caroline knew who it was without turning around.

"I don't mean to interrupt," Lisa said politely. "But, Matt, you offered your car if the Sadie Hawkins Committee needed it. We're going to have a meeting at my house and some of the gang needs a ride. Me included," she laughed. "Can you give us a lift?"

How long had Lisa been standing there? Caroline wondered. How much had she heard?

"Should we wait," Lisa asked tentatively, "while you finish your conversation?"

"No, that's okay. Caroline has to talk to a friend anyway. Don't you, Caroline?" Matt said.

Caroline knew Matt was hurt and striking out in anger but that didn't make her feel any better. She had too much pride to stand taking it. If he wants to think the worst of me then let him, she thought. Aloud she answered, "You're right. I do have to talk to a friend." She turned without another word, leaving Matt with Lisa and her friends.

Halloween was not a joyous holiday for Caroline. She carved a mournful expression on the pumpkin and planted it prominently in a center window.

On Halloween she joined her parents in handing out the treats to the little tricksters and played the yearly guessing game of pinning names to unrecognizable faces. She was doing all the right things in the hope no one would see how miserable she really was.

The weekend had started off badly enough with her fight with Matt. If that wasn't enough, the following day the Chargers lost their first game of the season. What first had seemed like a fairly easy Charger victory, even with Caroline on the bench, turned into a disaster when two of her teammates sustained injuries in quick succession. Val Davis was the first to fall victim with a sprained ankle, while another teammate was rushed to the hospital with a bump on her head the size of an avocado pit.

Caroline didn't get into the game until the third quarter but though she played her best, scoring eighteen points in less than two quarters of play, with the loss of two key players it was a losing battle. This wasn't exactly the way she envisioned the start of the season. But the way her life was going, she wasn't surprised.

She had had plenty of time to think about her last meeting with Matt. She felt she deserved an apology. And she determined to wait coolly for as long as it took until she got one. But she couldn't rule her emotions so easily. Each time the phone rang she jumped in anticipation. Each knock on the door accelerated her heartbeat. By Sunday she wondered if she would ever hear from Matt again.

November was ushered in by extreme cold. Roads iced over and cars required extra warm-up time before starting. Caroline was finding life depressing. The long, dreary days stretched out one after the other with little to mark them. She went through all the motions. She attended classes as usual and basketball practices as expected.

She even began to look forward to her tutorial time with David. He was a nice guy with a wild sense of humor, she quickly discovered, and he was good. Even she could understand his explanation of problems and formulas. As a result she was beginning to lose some of her fear of geometry. She even shocked Mr. Jeffers by answering a question in class one day and was pleased by his surprised smile. Slowly, her life began to look up in every way but one. She still had not heard from Matt.

Even her parents were beginning to question Matt's whereabouts and excuses that "he was busy too these days preparing for finals" or she "saw him after practice earlier" were beginning to sound pretty weak. She avoided any discussion of the Sadie Hawkins Dance. When her mother suggested shopping for a suitable dress, she sidestepped the issue and assured her there was plenty of time. Only Kurt seemed to have an inkling that something was wrong, but he kept his own counsel which was fine with Caroline. She wanted to solve her own problems without her parents' or big brother's help.

As the week passed the Glendale grapevine picked up on the rift between Caroline and Matt. She became aware of the interest she was generating. Buddies of Matt once cordial before seemed overly friendly to her now. No one mentioned Matt to her. Caroline knew she wasn't imagining the whispers that seemed to end quickly whenever she walked by a group of talkative females. It wasn't however, until the end of the week that Caroline heard something about Matt.

"Some of the kids are saying Matt's been working hard on the Sadie Hawkins Dance Committee," Sheila told her. Then she nearly exploded into tears. "Oh Caroline, I don't mean to hurt you, but I think you should know. They say Lisa Bentley stuck to Matt like glue at that concert you skipped and now it looks like it paid off. Some of the students are saying Matt and she are pretty chummy these days . . ."

It was all Caroline could do to stem the tears from flowing down her face. "I know it's not easy being the bearer of bad news," Caroline said. "But thanks anyway for telling me."

The remainder of the day seemed longer than usual for Caroline. Now it was finally time for blessed release. Only Amber was there to comfort her as she cried herself to sleep.

The weekend passed uneventfully, the harsh winter weather still in evidence. By Monday the Vickers household had its first casualty of the season. Mr. Vickers was flat on his back in bed with the flu.

"I'm going into the office today to take care of some paperwork; and to show a house," Mrs. Vickers told Kurt and Caroline. "I'll probably be filling in all week while your father is sick." She sighed. "I expect you both to pitch in."

"Think you can handle it at his office, mom?" Kurt asked.

"I'll have you know your father and I started that office. I guess I can just about remember the routine. Now look you two," she said as she pulled on her coat. "No monkeying around after school. Straight home, Kurt. Got me? Your father will be hungry and it'll be time for his medicine. I'll be home at lunch so

I'll look in on him then. When will you be getting home today, Caroline?" she asked.

"I have a game tonight, so it'll be close to seven I think. But I'll come home right afterward."

"Okay. I'll see you both later; and remember, get home as soon as you can. I may have to work late tonight."

Now life again became difficult for Caroline. In spite of the Chargers' first victory of the season, she knew she had not played her best. She had lost the ball twice and only scored six points. Her heart just wasn't into basketball these days—and it showed. She had wanted to talk to her father about Matt, but she thought it better not to worry him when he was sick. Finally she decided to take matters into her own hands. The opportunity presented itself sooner than she had expected.

"I can't make our meeting today," David informed Caroline hurriedly. "Is that going to be a problem? I can make it up tomorrow or this weekend if you like."

Caroline was so ecstatic she could have hugged him. "Whatever's good for you is okay with me. Give me a call later, okay?"

This was like a gift from heaven. Caroline had planned to talk to Matt in person, not over a phone, and now she had her chance. She'd see him after homeroom and get everything straightened out. For the first time in ages she cheerfully waited for the end of the day.

But by the time Caroline got to Matt's homeroom he was already gone. He has to be somewhere, she thought. As she walked down the hallway, she ran into a group of Matt's friends. Swallowing the lump in her throat she went up to them and asked for Matt.

"He's working at the stables after school this week." With a quick thanks Caroline raced off, not caring how it looked. One of the buses dropped students off right near Montgomery's. If she hurried she could just make it.

With books in hand, Caroline walked up the graveled path to the stables. She immediately recognized Matt's car at the end of a row of cars. Not seeing him in the front corral, she slowly walked around back and met Mr. Montgomery, his left arm in a sling. "Mr. Montgomery," she cried with concern, "are you all right? What did you do to yourself?"

"Just fine. Don't you worry. A little kick in the arm won't stop me, especially when I have the likes of your Matt to help me out." He winked.

Caroline could feel herself blushing. *Her* Matt? She didn't know if Matt was still hers or not. She hoped it wasn't too late to clear up a terrible mistake.

"I take it you're looking for him now," Mr. Montgomery smiled. "Last time I saw him he was heading toward the barn. That was a while ago though."

"Thanks," Caroline replied and sprinted off.

When she reached the barn door, she hesitated briefly. This was so important to her. She badly wanted to make everything as it had been between herself and Matt; now she didn't know what to say.

As she stepped into the barn she saw two figures at the far end. Matt and Lisa. Matt had his hands on Lisa's shoulder and Caroline saw him incline his head to kiss her. Caroline didn't wait to see any more. Half blind with tears, she ran out the barn door.

11

It was a long walk home from the stables. But it wasn't long enough for the numbness Caroline felt to wear off. Her face was drawn yet free from the tears she had shed earlier. She was past all point of caring for anything. All she wanted to do was to be by herself.

"And where have you been?" her mother asked pointedly as she stumbled into the house.

Not expecting such a sudden confrontation Caroline said the first thing that came to mind. "I had a tutorial with David. I guess we lost track of time."

"I guess *you* lost track of time. David called a little while ago and said he could meet you later this evening if you were interested." Mrs. Vickers gave her daughter a long hard look, then asked gently, "Caroline, where have you been? I've never known you to deliberately lie to me like that. What's wrong?"

Her mother's kindness was more than Caroline could bear. If only she knew the lies she had told her and her father! What would they think of her then? Despite her resolve, her tears flowed again. She flung herself into her mother's arms.

"Oh, Caroline, what's wrong? It can't be as bad as all that."

Between the tears and the sobs Caroline told her mother everything. About Matt and her compromises to make him happy. Her disappointment in herself. The pressure over her grades and sitting on the bench. Everything came tumbling out. By the time she was finished Mrs. Vickers was nearly as upset as her daughter.

"We all just assumed you were doing okay and could handle everything," Mrs. Vickers said. "You've always been so independent and strong."

"Oh, mom," Caroline cried helplessly. "Everything the kids said about Matt was true."

Taking her daughter in her arms once more,

Mrs. Vickers kissed her brow and held up her chin. "You'll go ahead and do what you have to do. You have your basketball, good friends, and work to do. I know you're disappointed and hurt but you're a survivor. The best thing for a broken heart is to keep busy, my mother always said. I'm afraid that's all I can say to you, baby. The rest is up to you."

Caroline wanted to skip classes the next day but a determined look from her mother and a little push sent her on her way. The effort she had to make to suppress her tears was a constant reminder of yesterday's unhappiness but Caroline tried not to let it overwhelm her. Her class participation was more restrained than usual. Not even Sheila or Beth knew how she felt. Caroline didn't volunteer any information. In time she would, but not now while the wound was raw and painful.

Afternoon basketball practice was a good long session and Caroline lost herself with the drills and scrimmages. By the time her laps were finished all she could think about was a shower and home. She collected her clothes, gym equipment, and books and hurried to catch her ride with Kurt.

She had just left the locker room when a voice spoke behind her. "Taxi."

Caroline turned to find herself facing Matt.

"My brother's waiting for me. I have to go," she said rudely, pushing past him.

"He *was* waiting for you. I told him I'd bring you home."

"You what! We have nothing to say to each other and I never want to see you again!"

"Wait," Matt said patiently as he grabbed her arm. "Your brother thought it was a good idea that I bring you home. Wouldn't you like to know why?"

Caroline tried to yank away her arm from his firm grasp.

"Caroline . . . there are so many things I want to say to you but first I guess I should apologize. I was wrong about you and David."

"You didn't even give me a chance to explain," she cried. "But what difference does it make now?"

"It makes a lot of difference if you'll only tell me why you ran away yesterday. I saw you as you left and called after you but you didn't stop."

Caroline sighed, "It seemed to me . . . you seemed to be busy."

"I was, but not in the way you thought. Lisa just happened to invite herself over. We'd been working closely on the Sadie Hawkins thing and she came by to ask me to go with her." He paused. "I told her I couldn't. She's a nice kid, but not my type. She got upset and I was telling her how sorry I was. I think she just wanted to know that I thought she was okay and if it weren't for you I would have gone with her."

Caroline couldn't believe what she was hearing.

"It was all a big mistake. It's just that . . ." Matt hesitated momentarily then looked directly into her eyes. "It's just that you're the only girl I really want to go to the dance with. I really care for you, although I never said so before. You're just so independent and direct that you scared me at first. Then as I got to know you I realized you were for real. It's not that other things in your life are more important than me—I'm sure of that now. But I had to learn they were *just as important* as me and you really weren't giving me the runaround. Does any of this make sense to you?"

A kiss on his cheek was her reply. Matt grinned, "Does that mean we're going to the dance?"

"Yes . . . but I wanted to ask you. You spoiled it," she teased.

"As long as we go together, who cares who asked whom?" He laughed and flipped her ponytail. "But if it'll make you happy the annual Winter Carnival is just around the corner and I'll be expecting you to ask me . . . deal?"

"Deal," she said, slipping her hand into his.

Hand in hand, they sauntered down the school corridor, too absorbed in each other even to notice Coach Cooper who was striding briskly ahead of them.

"I THINK I CAN! I THINK I CAN!" The Little Engine That Could had puffed valiantly up the hill. Caroline remembered her father's warm brown eyes sparkling as he had recited the words to her. And she could! Just as her mother had said, she had it all—basketball, good friends, work to do and now, best of all, *Matt*. As if he had guessed her thoughts, he squeezed her hand. Beneath her lashes, she stole a look at him and caught the kiss in his eyes.

Three exciting First Love from Silhouette romances yours for 15 days—_free!_

If you enjoyed this First Love from Silhouette® you'll want to read more! These are true-to-life romances about the things that matter most to you now—your friendships, dating, getting along in school, and learning about yourself. The stories could really happen, and the characters are so real they'll seem like friends.

Now you can get 3 First Love from Silhouette romances to look over for 15 days—absolutely free! If you decide not to keep them, simply return them and pay nothing. But if you enjoy them as much as we believe you will, keep them and pay the invoice enclosed with your trial shipment. You'll then become a member of the First Love from Silhouette℠ Book Club and will receive 3 more new First Love from Silhouette romances every month. You'll always be among the first to get them, and you'll never miss a new title. There is no minimum number of books to buy and you can cancel at any time. To receive your 3 books, mail the coupon below today.

First Love from Silhouette® is a service mark and a registered trademark of Simon & Schuster.

First Love from Silhouette

THERE'S NOTHING QUITE AS SPECIAL AS A **FIRST LOVE.**

$1.75 each
---

1 □ NEW BOY IN TOWN
Francis

2 □ GIRL IN THE ROUGH
Wunsch

3 □ PLEASE LET ME IN
Beckman

4 □ SERENADE
Marceau

5 □ FLOWERS FOR LISA
Ladd

6 □ KATE HERSELF
Erskine

7 □ SONGBIRD
Enfield

10 □ PLEASE LOVE ME . . .
SOMEBODY Johnson

11 □ IT'S MY TURN
Carr

12 □ IN MY SISTER'S SHADOW
Dellin

13 □ SOMETIME MY LOVE
Ryan

14 □ PROMISED KISS
Ladd

15 □ SUMMER ROMANCE
Diamond

16 □ SOMEONE TO LOVE
Bryan

17 □ GOLDEN GIRL
Erskine

18 □ WE BELONG TOGETHER
Harper

19 □ TOMORROW'S WISH
Ryan

20 □ SAY PLEASE!
Francis

21 □ TEACH ME TO LOVE
Davis

22 □ THAT SPECIAL SUMMER
Kent

$1.95 each
---

23 □ WHEN SEPTEMBER
RETURNS Jones

24 □ DREAM LOVER
Treadwell

25 □ THE PERSONAL TOUCH
Cooney

26 □ A TIME FOR US
Ryan

27 □ A SECRET PLACE
Francis

28 □ LESSON IN LOVE
West

29 □ FOR THE LOVE OF LORI
Ladd

30 □ A BOY TO DREAM ABOUT
Quinn

31 □ THE FIRST ACT
London

32 □ DARE TO LOVE
Bush

33 □ YOU AND ME
Johnson

34 □ THE PERFECT FIGURE
March

First Love from Silhouette

First Love from Silhouette

Look for These
New First Love Romances from
Silhouette Books Next Month

Just Friends

Dorothy Francis

The ultimate romance . . . moonlight and roses . . .
a boyfriend who would always remember her
birthday, ask her to all the big events . . . that's
what Jacey had always wanted. Had she chosen the
wrong guy? Or was this a different kind of love?

Promises To Come

Genell Dellin

What do you do when you fall for a boy and your
brothers call you "Red" and make you sound
immature and boyish? Should you give up playing
shortstop? Go wild with makeup? Flirt
outrageously? Only Tiffany knows for sure!

A Knight To Remember

Pam Martin

Tina was sure that proud Michael Donovan, the
handsome horse trainer, was unimportant in her
life. First came Stan, her steady boyfriend, and
then, Bell her horse. Why then, did he continue
riding through her dreams?

6 brand new Silhouette Romance novels yours for 15 days—Free!

If you enjoyed this Silhouette First Love, and would like to move on to even more thrilling, satisfying stories then Silhouette Romances are for you. Enjoy the challenges, conflicts, and joys of love. Sensitive heroines will enchant you—powerful heroes will delight you as they sweep you off to adventures around the world.

6 Silhouette Romances, free for 15 days!

We'll send you 6 new Silhouette Romances to keep for 15 days, absolutely free! If you decide not to keep them, send them back to us. You pay nothing.

FREE HOME DELIVERY. But if you enjoy them as much as we think you will, keep them by paying the invoice enclosed with your free trial shipment. You'll then automatically become a member of the Silhouette Book Club and receive 6 more new Silhouette romances every month.

There is no minimum number of books to buy and you can cancel at any time.